From The Convent To The Rawhide

The Saga Of
Sadie Cade And Vi Montana

Sage Sweetwater

Bloomington, IN Milton Keynes, UK

AuthorHouse™
1663 Liberty Drive, Suite 200
Bloomington, IN 47403
www.authorhouse.com
Phone: 1-800-839-8640

AuthorHouse™ UK Ltd.
500 Avebury Boulevard
Central Milton Keynes, MK9 2BE
www.authorhouse.co.uk
Phone: 08001974150

© 2006 Sage Sweetwater. All rights reserved.

No part of this book may be reproduced, stored in a retrieval system, or transmitted by any means without the written permission of the author.

First published by AuthorHouse 5/31/2006

ISBN: 1-4259-2633-9 (sc)

Library of Congress Control Number: 2006902522

Printed in the United States of America
Bloomington, Indiana

This book is printed on acid-free paper.

Sage Sweetwater, Firebrand Lesbian Novelist
http://www.authorsden.com/sagesweetwater

Sage Sweetwater Creative Properties
http://home.earthlink.net/~sagesweetwater/

Cover photo by Verna Bice
http://See-Our-Photos.com
jbice@brazosport.edu

Other books by Sage Sweetwater published by http://www.authorhouse.com
THE BUCKSKIN SKIRT OAR TRAVELER

About the Author

Sage Sweetwater revives lesbian pulp fiction adjusted to modern day. Sage Sweetwater's novels have a recurring formula, and fits the size of the dime store novel she applies to modern day lesbian fiction.

Unlike the yesteryear lesbian pulp fiction, imagery is not directed in the bedroom. Sage Sweetwater taps into the cultural pulse and weaves lesbian fiction from social, political, environmental, and religious themes.

Sage Sweetwater's creative properties are being represented in Hollywood for screen adaptation.

Introduction

Set in St. George, Utah and Clovis, New Mexico, *FROM THE CONVENT TO THE RAWHIDE: THE SAGA OF SADIE CADE AND VI MONTANA* is a modern-day feminist/lesbian Western where sex and religion ride together, converting from Mormonism to going Dreamtime in the Australian outback.

FROM THE CONVENT TO THE RAWHIDE: THE SAGA OF SADIE CADE AND VI MONTANA rides without "chaps." The author intends for it to be read in the wide open and not marked by chapters, staying with the theme of these cows which are not fenced in by barbed wire or branded — analogous of the perfect hides showing no scars — perhaps in search of the perfection of humans and simpler life.

The time frame of this novel skips back and forth, not to confuse Sage Sweetwater's readers, but the intermittence is structured as an alliance between contemplation, set-point, and one's mission in life, where it will all take one in the end, integrating it into one's own life, hopefully on a spiritual journey of happiness and wholeness.

FROM THE CONVENT TO THE RAWHIDE: THE SAGA OF SADIE CADE AND VI MONTANA is written for women with feminist/lesbian sensibilities in mind, hopefully allowing women to find the better part of them. The author certainly has, through writing this novel.

"It's time to get back to the size of the dime-store novels..."
(Sage Sweetwater).

In the '40s, '50s, and '60s, the purpose of dime-store novels was to lure working-class audiences. They were distributed at newsstands, dry goods stores, drug stores, and bus depots.

Dime-store novels typified Wild West stories, urban outlaws, detective stories, working-girl chronicles, and romances.

When you pair dime-store novels with lesbian pulp fiction of that same era, both having lurid cover illustrations, Sage Sweetwater novels have a recurring formula that fits the size of the dime-store novel she applies to modern-day lesbian fiction set in more positive times.

Unlike the yesteryear lesbian pulp fiction, imagery is not directed in the bedroom in Sage Sweetwater novels. Sage Sweetwater taps into the cultural pulse and weaves lesbian fiction from social, political, environmental, and religious themes with carefully chosen, uncensored lesbian sex scenes hot enough that no more than a few are needed.

There have been films based on lesbian pulps as well as dime-store Western novels by Louis L'Amour.

The most well-known vintage lesbian pulp fiction writers are Ann Bannon and Vin Packer. In their time, publishers insisted on moral endings to punish lesbian sexuality and at the same time, exploited it. Lesbian characters did not fare well in these novels and normally had to suffer downfalls to make up for being lesbian, a biased form of social punishment because lesbianism had no place in society. An example of this on a vintage lesbian novel cover reads *"What unholy bonds held two beautiful actresses in a drama that had no part for male actors? NEVER BEFORE PUBLISHED! A BRILLIANT NOVEL ABOUT THE LOVE SOCIETY RECOGNIZES BUT CANNOT FORGIVE!"*

Many of the lesbian pulp novels were written by men to stimulate other men. Lesbian characters were "saved by a man" and turned straight, ended up in institutions, became alcoholics, or committed suicide. Lesbianism could not be condoned in the pulp fiction novels in this era because it violated postal obscenity codes.

Lesbian pulp fiction novels of yesteryear are hot collectibles with the cover art bringing thousands of dollars.

Always with positive endings, Sage Sweetwater novels are based on a much deeper level than the dime-store novels or lesbian pulp fiction novels. This can be said because we live in a different time and place.

Come gather 'round me girls,
And I'll tell you a tale;

I left a lady in tears
And I said that
In a Western novel
Where sex and religion
Ride together;

Racing to control
Her spooked heart
Was only part of her troubles;

I quit her
In the monotony
Of the chase
And instead, bought
A handful of hearts,
Rough-hewn pewter,
Tokens of affection from
Sundance,
To tuck under my pillow.
Whoopee-ti-yi-yo!

Sister Pish is making jujube jam and jujube cough syrup. Even *Bailey's Encyclopedia of Horticulture* recommends the jujube to treat sore throats and fevers.

A grove of jujube fruit trees grows on the convent property where they thrive in dry soil. The jujube is such a heavy bearer that one tree alone can satisfy the tastes of many sisters at the Pish Convent in St. George, Utah.

Twenty-three Mormon nuns and seven "sister" missionaries ranging in ages from twenty-one to seventy maintain the 300-acre convent and grounds, which are open to guests.

Mercedes Cade is one of the missionaries here, trying to find her mission in life where the Pish Convent grants peace of mind and a contemplative atmosphere.

What Mercedes needs to do is find her "set-point." Everyone has a set-point for happiness, and a person's average level is almost always inherited, but that doesn't mean we are stuck with the levels nature gave us. We can rise above our set-points and act in ways that encourage happiness and wholeness. What is important is how frequently we are happy, not how intensely. The peaks of happiness — being swept off our feet in love's doorway, climbing "fourteeners," or winning the lottery are all nice, but happiness comes down to being serenely content on an even level.

It isn't uncommon to find a nun driving a tractor or milking a cow. They raise beef to supplement the economy of the simple convent.

Before going to the retreat house for breakfast prepared by the nuns, Mercedes rises before the sun, showers, and dresses in a navy blue skirt that falls to mid-calf and a white blouse that covers her cleavage — the strictly enforced code of modesty for a missionary. Like every day, this morning starts with a song and a prayer.

For eighteen months, Mercedes will be required to put in fourteen-hour days. She is to give up simple indulgences such as television or newspapers, and is allowed absolutely no telephones to call relatives or friends. Mail is the only way to keep in contact.

After a hearty breakfast, Mercedes and her "sister" missionary head off for "field teaching," or knocking on doors, the trademark of the Mormon missionary in a way to get the word out. Missionary rules require that they hit the road by 9:30 AM. This outing is grounded in a rule where they must always travel in pairs and must always remain within earshot of each other.

Mercedes and Annie carry a special spirit. Besides traveling to distant neighborhoods to introduce strangers to the Mormon faith, they are also required to perform eight hours of volunteer service weekly.

All in all, today goes well; there's a little of everything: A few doors are slammed in their faces; some say they aren't interested; some are practicing another religion; and some are atheist. One resident tells them they can come back later, and a nice family invites them in for decaffeinated tea and bagels, saying they will browse their pamphlets.

At noon, they take their brown-bag lunch under the jujube trees back at the convent. It is Annie's last day. Her eighteen months are up and Mercedes will be paired up with another sister. It's just how it works out, not all of their arrival dates are at the same time, so there are always some who have more time.

"I'll miss you, Annie," Mercedes says, knowing when it is over, it is *over*, unless the missionary wants to take her vows to be a Sister with a capital S. The missionary "sisters" are addressed less authoritative with a lowercase *s*.

Annie is going back to finish her senior year at the University of Arkansas. "I only wished I could be closer to visit," Annie says, already missing the totality of the little things that add up.

"You'll write then?" Mercedes asks. "And send pictures?"

"Sure. The work here was fulfilling. I enjoyed volunteering at the food pantry the most, and I will never forget these jujube trees and their heavenly fruit." The jujubes smell like Christmas, their spicy scent wafting in the autumn air. Sister Pish puts up many jars, some red with cinnamon, others green with mint, and crocks of jujube jam, delicious paired with peanut butter sandwiched in between two slices of bread. "Shake that tree, I want to take some back with me," Annie says of the fruit shaped like a small plum with a skin like a yellow apple, perhaps created from a seed in the Garden of Eden evolving into the "fruit of celibacy" when temptation waxes.

The Mormon Church urges chastity. "Resist temptation and stay away from premarital sex," then ninety-year-old Gordon B. Hinckley, Mormon Church president, told a gathering of female members. "You have within you instincts, powerful and terribly persuasive, urging you at times to let go and experience a little fling. You must not do it," he says. "Young Mormon women should educate themselves, in case they have to earn a living."

The tenets of Mormonism demand heavy commitment. Mormons are expected to abstain from alcohol, tobacco, caffeine, gambling, and premarital sex.

The Pish Convent is a privately-owned community for nuns. Sister Pish has owned the homestead for forty-some years. She planted just a single row of a dozen jujube seedlings the Department of Agriculture gave her for experimental purposes, and they have grown so well over the years they now spread wide enough to border one side of God's little green acre.

Keeping with the tenets of Mormonism, Sister Pish gives her tithe — 10 percent of her gross annual income — to the Mormon Church in Salt Lake City.

Guests pay $50 for the first twenty-four hours and $20 for each successive day. The rooms are simple, each about ten by fifteen. There is one bed, one study table with a lamp, and one closet. The community bathroom is shared and there is absolutely no electronic communication. That means no cell phones, pagers, or laptops. Guests are required to supply their own food. Towels and bedding are supplied, as well as a furnished community kitchen.

Most of those who come are those who want time away from metropolis — a serene place where they can read a book by a stream, knowing they are in a spiritual atmosphere, regardless whether they are Mormon or not. Some aren't affiliated with any organized religion — it doesn't matter as long as you honor those here who are. Sister Pish welcomes everyone, as long as they abstain from alcohol, tobacco, caffeine, gambling, and premarital sex while they are on her divine property.

Sadie Cade and Vi Montana point and laugh at the spiritual pair of black and white birds with navy tail feathers. "Remind you of anything?" Sadie asks. "The magpies are flying to distant neighborhoods for 'field teaching.' The bird is dressed in the code of missionary modesty just like her sister, their white 'blouses' covering their chest up to their bobbing chins."

"I wonder what her religion is," Vi comments, looking at her watch. It is 9:30 AM.

"Worm Underground religion," Sadie jests. "It's for early birds."

"Oh, you're good, cowgirl," Vi laughs. "Damn good!" Yes indeed. Each magpie unearths her breakfast for much-needed energy to bring in some converts this morning. "Go get them!"

They are mounted on their horses, the palomino and paint, well-groomed and well-tended. Every morning at 9:30, they go out into the field to check on their hides. Their Brahman-cross herd is not fenced in or branded. Sadie and Vi run a mid-sized leather ranch with top-of-the-line gene pool, bred for their perfect hides. These cows show no scars. The natural grains of their unflawed hides are highly valued by leather furniture consumers who buy the best leather, paying for perfection and the coddled lifestyle of the cow.

Their "field" is a thousand-some acres in Clovis, New Mexico where the cows have plenty of acres to graze freely. When the herd strays a little farther out than Sadie or Vi feels comfortable with, they push them back into range.

Yucca is native to much of the West, and is designated as the state flower of New Mexico. It can be a wonderful help in horse training to those who live where this long, tough-needle plant grows.

Sadie and Vi trained their horses quite some time ago by riding up to the yucca and reining their horses back and forth in front of it, then moving them closer to the yucca so that the sharp needles would poke the horses' front legs. This isn't cruel, but rather makes the horses watch where they are going. It is just good basic training and they never work either of their mounts over five minutes a day on a yucca. The horses don't like the yucca stinging their legs, and hitting the yucca a few times teaches the horses to lift their front legs over the "Spanish Dagger" instead of through it.

Vi's palomino has began drifting out of its stops recently, so she took it back to the yucca to be tuned. She lopes the filly straight at the yucca and asks her to stop a few feet from the yucca. The filly gets her hindquarters under her for a sliding stop, cutting her slide short by coming to a nice, solid stop to keep her sliding into the yucca. "Well done, girl."

These two ladies in denim blue know hunting for cattle requires patience. If you push cattle too hard, the mamas lose their calves in the springtime – and then stop, turn around and bawl for them – and if you push them too hard in the fall to come down from the hills, they scatter off the trail and you have to go after them and set them right. There is just no sense in being impatient in any season of religion, because if you are, you are bound to miss a few and have to go back sometimes, and others are bound to drift into the areas you have already "cleaned."

Compare the reward of time well spent learning and gathering life's knowledge, communicating with one another individually and as a family, rather than wasted time in a room viewing excessive television. To those needing to wean themselves from television, start by muting the volume when the overdone pharmaceutical advertisements come on (this includes *Viagra!* We're going *down*, not up!) And the commercials immediately after these: the attorneys who want you to join in a lawsuit if you have experienced any side-effects from those pharmaceuticals that were just advertised. Mute every bathroom product commercial too – because even when they're muted, they make too much noise – and completely turn off the set when *"you can't believe it's not butter"* (Fabio's not such a pretty boy.) After a few times of this, it will become quite clear that you're glad you're a lesbian and don't have to deal with the things straight married women do, that the too-old-to-dispense-the-mustard kitchen aids and the marital aids are one in the same and the straight women will decide there are better ways to spend their time. Everyone has a "breaking point" just like everyone has a "set-point."

Twelve months to go; Mercedes Cade has put in six months at the Pish Convent, making good use of her time. Little by little, she is gaining her set-point.

Pipe organs are elemental creations of earth and air, touch, and spirit. They are paintings in sound and they make space come alive in the Church of Pish. Sister Pish's church on the grounds of the convent is an acoustic masterpiece. Sitting quietly on the pews, turning the pages of the hymnals sound like hailstones pounding the steel milking pails. It is no exaggeration; sound is gloriously magnified in this church.

It is just fascinating to Mercedes that the pipe organ produces such heavenly music, from the deep thunder of a flue pipe as big as a water heater to the quack of a reed pipe as tiny as a pencil.

She has made a nice acquaintance with Mr. Linhart, who builds and repairs pipe organs. Studiously, Mercedes listens and learns about this marvelous instrument, which has sadly been replaced with digital and synthesized instruments, acoustic organs supplemented with "electronic" pipes. Electronic society has also found its way into modern-day religion, where churches are choosing to be retrofitted with digital sampling gear to supplement the pipes.

"Only purists can distinguish the difference," Mr. Linhart tells her. "They aren't imitating our sound; they are *stealing* it," he says, "and ruining it."

He explains to her that the electronic sounds are pipe-by-pipe recordings of great organs played through speakers rather than air moving through highly individualistic acoustical instruments. This is where Mrs. Linhart comes in. She repairs the small leather pouches that allow air into organ pipes when the keys are pressed.

Restoring a pipe organ costs from $50,000 to one million or more, and a newly built pipe organ starts at $250,000, while a new electronic organ costs $40,000 to $50,000, a fraction of the price. It's why some churches are opting for the electronic organs, but the electronic components and plastic keys wear out over about twenty-five years, whereas the pipe organs can give a century or two of life.

It is here where Mercedes learns to appreciate Mozart. Mormon missionaries can only listen to classical music written before 1800. Classical composers excelled in Christian music. In Mozart's day, musicians wanting to earn a good income had two options. They could work for people of the highest social level — who commissioned compositions for special occasions — or for the clergy, as Mozart's father did in Salzburg. Mozart, however chose to go at it alone, becoming one of the full-fledged classical freelancers, which meant a hand-to-mouth existence that left him penniless at the time of his death, when he was buried in an unmarked pauper's grave in Vienna.

Mozart kept his religion a private matter. He was a devout Catholic and many of his compositions were the result of the sacred vows he made privately with God. One such religious masterpiece was the *C Minor Mass*. Mercedes loves hearing the organist play it. When she hears it, she goes beyond the human dimension and enters the mystery of bliss through the pitch of the pipes set in their openings, giving them their unique medieval sound.

Mercedes has her own special time in the evening; it is when she does her letter-writing. She writes to her mother on a weekly basis.

> I am not pursuing this Missionary work as an occupation. I am truly here to learn about spiritual happiness, and in going about my daily duties provide me with enjoyment I will take with me when

I leave the Pish Convent. The wonders of nature are all around me and I have room for the wide range of emotions that the city constricts. I have my window open and I can smell the spicy scent of the jujube trees just a few acres west of my room. I am in search of honest, hard work, and finding appreciation for the simpler things. These grounds are to remind me of the beauty of God's creation. Please know that I am in a place of peace, Love Always, Mercedes.

For Mercedes, the decision to become a missionary was not obvious to her mother. When she announced that she was going away for eighteen months to a convent, her mother was surprised. Mercedes was raised in the Latter-day Saints Church, but it was never one of her favorite things. Only a little over six months ago — a few days after her thirty-eighth birthday — did she feel a great leaning toward reuniting with the church through missionary work. It isn't because of her testimony or belief, but rather finding her place in life by the time she is forty, a time in a woman's life when she becomes closest to her spirituality and a wellspring of creativity flows, where wonderful things begin to happen.

An unmarried woman may be glad that she doesn't have to put up with an uncooperative husband or live in a noisy, messy home with her children, considering how noise pollution will affect her health and nervous system. She may honestly prefer peace and quiet, and be glad that she doesn't have to bring up teenagers in modern-day society, but she also has anxious moments wondering whether she may be more alone in the future than now. Who will be concerned about her when she grows old? Where will there be a companion to share her retirement? What will happen to her if she should become ill and who will be there to care for her?

Not much attention has ever been paid to the American cowgirl. We always have thought of the lonesome cowboy strumming *his* guitar at sunset with only *his* horse for company. But history shows that women of the West helped tame it; Calamity Jane and the Lady Wildcats, Belle Starr, Annie Oakley, Lottie Deno, "the Gambling Queen of Hearts," the Dalton women (in particular), Eugenia Moore, Julia Johnson, and the Rose of Cimarron, to name a few.

The "early cowgirl" was perhaps our first professional woman athlete. From 1900 to 1929, during the early years of rodeo, women were allowed to perform the same events as men; they rode bulls and broncs, and wrestled steers. It wasn't until 1930 that the women mostly stopped competing in these dangerous events, after Bonnie McCarrol's death in 1929 from being thrown from a bucking horse. They competed in relay race competitions and exhibitions at rodeos, later racing around barrels, the popular modern-day women's rodeo sport. The first lady to be called a "cowgirl" is a woman by the name of Lucille Mulhall. It was Will Rogers who first called a cowgirl a "cowgirl."

Changing times and changing economics are doing away with Western traditions. The cowgirl is vanishing from the land where corporate mergers are taking the land; however, two cowgirls in Clovis, New Mexico are alive and well; Sadie and Vi owe their existence to scarce water. It is ironic but true, that people always settle where there is the sweetest water, and the farmer and rancher get pushed aside into marginal

From The Convent To The Rawhide

areas. So the best land always gets covered by concrete and asphalt. Waterless lands virtually prove inhabitable unless one puts up a windmill when they spot a water source, perhaps where a patch of green clover sprouts out in the middle of arid nowhere, or another sign is where the cow-hoof tracks are filled with little oblong pools from a new spring.

Vi doesn't complain about the job — that of a "windmill monkey." The open gears of the mills need greased twice a week. She climbs the wooden tower with a grease gun in her holster. Atop the twenty-foot platform at the top, soaring above it is a restored wooden wheel, twenty-two-and-a-half feet in diameter.

"Come on up and give me a hand," Vi says.

Where one goes, the other one follows.

Windmill-pumped water from underground fills the stock tank. Each revolution of the wheel produces one up-and-down stroke of the pump rod. It takes considerable wind to make the wheel turn. Their particular model is the Eclipse. It is said that the Plains Indians removed the crescent-moon shaped weights, claiming the moon lost water, a result of the blades being turned down, meaning rain would not fall.

Their shiny belt buckles hang from the tower, dangling in the wind. "I want you, cowgirl," Vi says, pivoting the large vane to control the speed. Like a chugging steam-powered locomotive, Vi has an insatiable thirst and the windmill is the only device in sight that can slake it. Staying true to the original "railroad" model windmill, which the railroads bought in the 1800s to pump large quantities of water for their steam engines, Vi employs it in the most feminist way where she has her own ways of lubrication. Whir, creak, thunk, splash — not the sounds we ordinarily associate with orgasm, but those noises are music to their ears — these sounds *sucking* forth life-giving water from beneath arid plains.

All the early railroads had the Eclipse windmills spaced up and down the tracks, about thirty miles apart. Then, the

Eclipse name was as well-known as Stetson or Winchester. The windmills began disappearing with the advent of rural electricity, public water suppliers, and diesel-engine locomotives.

It is comforting to know the windmill is alive and well here on *these* acres. As a symbol of the American frontier, the windmill reminds us that the simpler way of life is not completely gone, where old ways should be kept alive not because they are old, but because they *work*, and where slow and steady still wins out over fast and electronic. It's when these values die, that we will be gone too – gone with the wind.

Sister Pish brings the new sister to Mercedes' cottage and introduces the two of them.

"I'm glad I was partnered with someone who looks to be close to my own age," the woman says.

Her name is Violet. She wipes the lipstick from her lips, blotting them with a tissue, remembering where she is now. There is no rule against wearing makeup here; Sister Pish does, lightly. She has such a pale complexion, especially in the fall. She always wears a straw bonnet to protect her face from melanoma, which runs in Sister Pish's "family," as does a sense of humor.

"There's nothing more disgraceful to God than a wrinkled nun," Sister Pish says. "Our faces have to look as pressed as our skirts."

"Are you ready to go out and bring in some converts this morning?" Mercedes asks.

"I want to bring two in today, this is my goal, then four, six, eight..."

Violet cheers. "I'll appreciate."

"Were you a cheerleader in high school?" Mercedes laughs.

"No, increments of two just work for me," Violet says.

"C'mon, I know an old country road which forks off two ways. As you like, we'll start off your first day in increments of two," Mercedes says, handing Violet two pamphlets outlining the tenets of the Mormon faith. They will talk about the six main principles: God, Jesus Christ, God's plan as revealed to the prophets, Joseph Smith (who was the organizer of the church), the Book of Mormon, and the Holy Ghost.

Mercedes drives out of St. George city limits toward Leeds. Utah has its own beauty — temperate climate, spiritual rock formations, and close-knit groups of people in touch with Zion, their promised land in the Great Basin, a sacred place.

"The Mormons believe that God and Jesus appeared before fourteen-year-old Joseph Smith in upstate New York in 1820. When the boy asked which church he should join, he was told to join none because all were wrong. Three years later, an angel named Moroni appeared before Joseph Smith and showed him a set of golden plates which ..." Violet proselytized, presenting the newcomer to the Mormon faith. "Can we count upon you to come to our church at the Pish Convent on Sunday?"

"Yes, we will come and listen," the woman says.

"Thank you for your time. The directions are printed on the back of the pamphlet," Violet says. "See the both of you on Sunday. God bless."

"Thank you," Mercedes says to the woman and her daughter, amazed at how well Violet knows her stuff. "I'll bet you look pretty in your Sunday dress," she tells the little girl.

"It pink, wif ruffews. It in da wash," the two-year-old girl says.

"Tell them what you spilled on it," her mother says just to hear her say it.

"Musood," she grins a smiley mustard face; cute.

There is a silence in the car, Violet pleased with her first contact and Mercedes speechless from Violet's brand of teaching — articulate and versed, but yet, contrived; not a bad thing.

"How far back was your fork in the road?" Mercedes asks Violet. "I'm curious." Almost everybody remembers a "fork in the road" experience in their life where one can trace events, accidents, whims, and decisions that made their lives better. Some are just mere coincidences, others odd twists of fate, and some of the miracle work of the Divine Providence. Later, they blossomed into decisions that made a profound difference in one's life. Do you remember yours?

"If that means the blessings of life dished out to everyday people," Violet answers, smooth-spoken, "like the politician who discovered the rats in a maze, I would say that only recently have I discovered my fork in the road."

They drive the back roads admiring the Dixie National Forest and the majestic stone spires and red-rock outcroppings shaped like thrones and temples, geographically and architecturally conjoined to the Mormon religion where Mormons followed Joseph Smith's successor Brigham Young to Utah. Indeed, they had chosen a promised land; *Zion*.

"A walk through a labyrinth sent me in a new direction," Violet says. "You go to these places with a personal conflict and you come out with a resolution."

Labyrinths are circular passageways needed to meditate or ponder difficult decisions. The ancient tool for prayer has been rediscovered by a new generation of spiritual seekers who are seeking a world without the stress of cellular phones, and by others who don't feel comfortable exploring their faith through traditional religious channels.

The labyrinth dates back to pre-Christian times and spans all cultures. It is not tied to any particular cause or

From The Convent To The Rawhide

any particular religion, but to human beings, central to spirituality.

The kabala or *Tree of Life* in the Jewish tradition is an elongated labyrinth figure based on the number eleven. The Hopi medicine wheel is based on the number four. Tibetan sand paintings — though not walked — are *mandalas*, a kind of labyrinth created through a meditative state, focusing on the spiritual center.

The oldest known labyrinths — the Cretan or seven-circuited labyrinths — date back more than 4,000 years. Early Roman-style labyrinths were made from mosaic tiles. In Christianity, one of the earliest labyrinths appeared on a wall at St. Lucca Cathedral in Italy. This labyrinth was designed for its parishioners to trace their fingers before they entered the cathedral as a way to quiet their minds before entering a sacred space.

Labyrinths are made of various materials. The Middle Age mazes in England were made of turf cut to reveal the underlying white chalk of chalklands. Modern-day labyrinths are constructed from concrete, stone, and cloth, and are found in private backyards, rolled out in religious centers, hospitals, prisons, parks, retreat centers, and airports across the globe.

Labyrinths have only one path to the center and back out. They are a metaphor for life, complete with unexpected turns, obstacles, and going at one's own pace, a one-way path that requires faith and patience. Whatever happens on that path happens.

The labyrinth walk is viewed in three parts; purgation, illumination, and union. The first stage signifies letting go of daily stresses, as the participant walks toward the center. The second stage signifies closeness with God as the walker reaches the center, and in the third stage, the labyrinth walker walks away from the center, signifying a new life of walking with God.

Violet has walked the labyrinth, one of the several set up on the East Lawn of Capitol Hill in Washington, D.C. called

"Labyrinths for Peace 2000," which was not about making a political statement. The temporary labyrinths are made of tape and surveyor flags set up to encourage politicians to find an inner peace so we can find world peace.

"I knew when I put one foot in front of the other and took my first step into the labyrinth, it was a path of change," Violet tells Mercedes. "Politicians aren't nourished in their routes of policy-making, but are criticized at every road, and then there are the unwashed politicians ..."

"Why were you at the Capitol?" Mercedes asks.

"Getting some laws on the books. You might know me from newspapers, radio, or television — Violet Mace-Reese, Democrat, House of Representatives, rebel lawmaker from Montana," she says.

"You're Violet Mace-Reese! I've heard of you just like you said. I didn't recognize you. Women's rights, child protection advocate, endangered species, gay rights, water rights, conservation easements, snowmobile pollution in Yellowstone... should I go on?"

"Please don't," Violet laughs, "you're a fan."

"You better believe it. I've appreciated all of your work even though I'm not from your state. Every time I heard or read anything controversial about you, I said, 'Now there's a woman who knows what's going on in the world and it's her ink on the books that will pave the way for other lady lawmakers,'" Mercedes says, giving her praise.

"That's such a nice compliment. And I'm happy to say that women are expected to be the majority of students entering law school in the fall," Violet says.

According to the American Bar Association, more women than men have applied for admission to law schools. In previous years, women were 46 percent of the entering class at Harvard Law School, 44 percent at Stanford Law School, 51 percent at Columbia Law School, and 50 percent at New York State University School of Law.

The trend is expected to help propel more women into leadership positions in politics and business, further serving as a springboard to positions of power. Several factors are driving the increase: security, income, prestige, and how modern-day women are reacting to barriers for women's rights, gaining a voice through politics.

"Moroni appeared before Joseph Smith and showed him a set of golden plates, which Joseph Smith translated. That text became to be known as the *Book of Mormon*. It tells of Christ administering in America after his resurrection. The book was published in 1830, launching the Mormon Church. The Mormons made several moves because they were under persecution and opposition. Joseph Smith was killed in Carthage, Illinois in 1844. Brigham Young was his successor. His followers moved to Utah to Zion, the promised land," Violet ended the primer on Mormonism with a brief church history. "Will you join us in worship on Sunday?"

Furniture starts with a frame, mostly made of wood. Quality furniture is made from hardwoods such as oak, alder, birch, and maple. These woods are strong and resilient, their tight grain holding pegs, screws, and nails securely in place for a long time.

After the frame is constructed, the choice of padding is pondered; what to pad the seat with after the coil springs are attached?

Almost everyone recognizes Spanish moss — in movies and paintings — where moss festoons oaks or drapes the cypress trees in snake-infested swamps.

Cured and dried, the moss was once used for stuffing horse collars, seat cushions, and upholstered furniture.

Trailering the horses, Sadie and Vi drive across the border to Texas to harvest Spanish moss for the padding in their old way of furniture-making to make a soft surface and conceal the feel of the springs and wood framing.

It is a holiday on horseback. Mountain Time turns into Central Time. The whole moss-gathering scene is canvas-friendly — why we ask ourselves why when men paint feminine subjects, that they're called gentle and admired, but when women "paint" soft scenes like this one, we are berated and tongue-lashed with derogatory tags, "*cunt licker*" and "*pussy licker*," rather than the proud "anatomical oralists" that we are. Yesterday's women had to be twice as good as a man to get half as far, but today's woman is catching up (she's right on your ass!) and it is a peaceable scene like this one why women convert. The modern-day attraction to lesbianism acknowledges at the same time that while she is empowering herself, she is exchanging her sexual preference. To apply a feminist Western metaphor, if the "horse" doesn't fit the job, change the "horse," *not* the job; not the conventional definition of the word, but well-suited, ladies, if the "shoe" fits, wear it, *convert*, as it applies to you.

Sadie and Vi locate an intense feeling at Muleshoe on the banks of the Black Water River where they spot their first oaks festooned in Spanish moss. They quit the horses when they spot the remnant of an ancient hearth eroding on an arroyo bank. When their trained eyes catch sight of a small quarry of chert, the prized stone they flint-knap their spearheads from, they want to explore it further on "canvas" and journey with it. Their canvas is the Aussie bedroll called a swag.

"Years ago, I chose to focus on the landscape because I have always felt a likeness toward them," Vi says. "My rebel spirit is part of nature, the outlaw prairies, the lawless mountains; the physical dynamics of the river, wild and opinionated as it cuts its own path, never minding the government, the rogue trees, even the sky is entertainment for a rebel lawmaker, its *cool* attitude with colorful exchanges, blue for pink, and azure for dove gray. All of it damn powerful like a rebel," Vi says, with her thoughts about all of it exchanged for words in authoritative prose. It is on the books, too, preserving the crumbling roads in Glacier National Park in Montana where there are beautiful lakes, rivers, deep valleys, peaks for fifty glaciers, bears, and spiritual gray wolves, and Yellowstone National Park, stretching from Wyoming across to Montana and Idaho where there are geysers, hot springs, pristine lakes, waterfalls, free-roaming bison, bears, and reintroduced gray wolves who frighten most, but the real threat is the snowmobiles causing pollution — noise and air — which Vi has traced, signing in ink on the books, the development of the conservation ethic.

"You can build a religion around this," Sadie tells Vi. Although particularly compatible with the "oak" religion, Spanish moss is universal in its choice of habitats. The early French settlers called it "Spanish Beard" and Spaniards in return, called it "French wig." Indians' translation for it was "long hair." Vi calls it "Rebel Flag."

Spanish moss thrives where there is water, on high humidity mostly in lowland swamps and river basins. It is said both painters and photographers find it impossible to capture because of its ever-changing look. Neither canvas nor film seem suited to reflect the play of light on the soft, gray-green strands, making it look too stiff, failing to catch the way it drifts gently in a soft breeze or tosses wildly in a storm. It takes two women harvesting it to capture its ethereal drapery and its many moods. It just does, and a feminist/lesbian writer to capture its play of light through *their play* through the imagery of the written word, "*word painting*" we call it, the medium which captures it best.

Harvesting Spanish moss is easy. They make it simple by fastening pieces of barbed wire to long poles, then shoving them into the streamers of moss to collect it, twirling it like spaghetti on a fork. The streamers blow softly like angel hair pasta, colored green like spinach. You know how it kind of clumps and strings together when you haul it to your mouth? That's the same way it responds. They haul the snarled strands down to the ground in a tangled mass of moss, some of the older plants reaching twelve feet.

Sadie and Vi pull down their "stuffing", and the moss, too, and heap it, their clothes and the moss in piles. After a night of swag and "bush telly" — slang for the Aussie campfire — they'll ride back for the truck and trailer and come back for it. In this quantity, it is hard to pack the volume out on horseback, especially if it is wet, which makes it very heavy.

The soft light of the bush telly overlaps territories and religions. Sadie and Vi go *Dreamtime* — where, in Australia's outback, the Creation myth tells of how the land was first shaped by the Sky Heroes, during the period before human memory, when supernatural beings roamed the land, spoke to them through a crocodile-like caiman in the mud, eyeing the stacks of Spanish moss, in a crock's eyes, (they have nictitating membranes, "third eyelids") a good place to stash its kill until it rots because they can't chew very well, tearing off chunks at their leisure.

On the bank of the Black Water River, playing in the heaps of Spanish moss, Sadie and Vi wrestle each other like rogue crocs — the "salties," massive saltwater crocs of Australia. Sadie has a habit of lying with her legs spread and her jaws agape like a crocodile, but not so innocent. A crocodile has to use more muscles to close its jaws than to open them, not so innocent of a pose for Sadie. Vi crawls in between Sadie's legs and eats her from the waist down, swallowing her salty crocodile tears.

"Snatch me good!" Sadie cries, asking Vi if she would drop to her knees in the *billabongs*, strings of pools, and stalk the croc poachers and close down the hide market if she was a rebel Aussie politician.

"Damn right, mate!" *Whomp!* Vi's jaws clamp down on Sadie's cunt. "Good saltie, nothing like it in the world; *Nothing!*" Vi drools, not missing a lick.

"Tucker for a croc," Sadie says, coming out of nowhere, flipping Vi on her back. *Plop!* She does have a taste for wild pink meat; Saltie: Nothing like it in the world. *Dreamtime* gone; A fuck in the billabong, swagging out under the stars of the Lone Star state, below the rogue oaks festooned with "Rebel Flag." How much more of a candid description of capturing the play of light on Spanish moss does one need! "Word painting," we call it.

"No use crying over spilled milk, Sister Cade," Sister Pish laughs. The cow kicked over the half-full milk pail. Mercedes can't say "Damn it!" But she thinks it. She worked hard to get that half-bucket. "Where morning glories twine around the door!" she says instead. Cows don't give milk, you have to take it from them. Just squeezing a teat isn't going to get it drawn out. You have to know how to work your fingers, knead and pull, knead and pull.

"Pray, my sister, for another bucket of milk," Sister Pish advises. "You need a poem for times like these." And so Sister Pish tells Mercedes a comical poem about all the different positions one can be in for praying. It ends up with someone falling into a well and praying upside down.

"Thank you, Sister Pish. I think now that I am not in such bad shape. Do we have a well on these acres, so I can be sure to stay a bit away from it while I am praying?" Humoring Sister Pish at daybreak keeps you in the good graces of the one in the Big Sky. "Thank you, God, for this pail I am about to fill." It all makes sense; sure it does. In our personal fruition, we naturally become pail-carriers of the Holy Spirit's life-sustaining refreshment to thirsty ones around us.

The rebel politician sat out under the jujubes meditating on the small, hand-held ceramic labyrinth she brought with her for walking the labyrinth in her mind.

When she walked the labyrinth at the capital, she hit many dead ends, so she made it more challenging by crawling through it, or "womb-walking." Hitting dead ends is a personal metaphor for her. Perhaps her political career has played itself out. That's what she is here for – to ask God for direction, in a place of tranquility needed for contemplative prayer and reflection now that she has finished out her political term and saved money for her mission.

She meditates in prophetic terms of the environment. Religious and spiritual believers are asked to be stewards of the environment. Being a lawmaker, she has encouraged people of all faiths to take responsibility for God's environment. "Think as manager of air, water, and land. They are gifts from God just like animals to be nurtured and respected throughout all stages of life," telling them if they are truly concerned about what God has created, they would ride a bike or take a bus to work instead of driving a car, and that they would recycle every newspaper, every can, and every bottle that their hands touched.

Religious groups need to learn how to make their churches and temples more energy efficient, because environmental action is a moral and righteous cause. The Bible begins with the creation story in Genesis and speaks clearly of human responsibility to care for that creation.

Utah is one such place where there is a mighty spiritual aspect to be found in the landscape, a place where the state's parks – Arches, Canyonland, Capitol Reef, Bryce Canyon, and Zion – dominate the calendar, postcard, and coffee-table-book trade, the basis for any valid religion, and speaks in

From The Convent To The Rawhide

languages from all over the world from foreign tourists who have been coming to Utah for years to let their mind wander down philosophical and religious paths.

Violet also meditates on the spiritual redemption through the Convention on International Trade in Endangered Species of Wild Fauna and Flora. The wife of an outgoing American ambassador to New Delhi, India has turned in her *shatoosh* shawl. The *shatoosh* – a luxurious wrap made from the throat fur of the endangered Tibetan antelope (all of it at the expense of slaughtering three to five of the antelope called *chirus*) – is fine enough that it can pass through a size-five ring, and each is worth between $2,000 to $15,000. Laws signed in Violet's and her constituents' ink made it illegal to purchase or sell *shatoosh* shawls in the United States and India.

It is most likely due to the politicians in Utah signing laws on noise pollution why Violet can meditate in *quiet* here on God's little green acres. Mechanized recreation has seized nine-tenths of the woods and forests. Violet has something to say about that in her own state of Montana where under the Wise Use dogma, portions of Montana's wilderness is "silenced" from the noisy motorboats that are only allowed in certain waters. Canoes instead are paddled along those same routes of the Indians where one can hear the lapping of water, bird songs, and wind in the trees. The way of the canoe was the way of the wilderness in simpler days where those who lived in these "quieter" years *had* to pursue the sounds, scents, and visions for their survival. Imagine being "drowned" out by Vrooom, putt, full-throttle, ZZzzzzzzzzz! You can't hear a cantankerous old bear coming out of a sleepy hollow up around the next bend, and you darn sure can't *smell* the bear with too many gas fumes stinking up the air.

Motorized watercrafters – operators of internal combustion engines are ignorant – unaffected by the wilderness activists who thrive on the silence of navigating by canoe. American democracy is built on compromise. In

Violet's opinion, the bills need to decrease the amount of water surface open to motorboats. She also fights to close 50 percent of the commercial motorized portages to limit overcrowding.

Clean water is scarce. Ballot initiatives are intended to put the guilty on the spot. Penalize the sugar companies in Florida for polluting the Everglades — charge so-much-a-pound fee on the region's sugar cane to pay for undoing damage to the Everglades water system — is heavily supported by the well-organized, well-funded committees supported by the National Audubon Society and the Florida Audubon Society.

Purity of anything in modern-day life is hard to come by. We are hearing constantly about the energy crisis. Violet is fed up with sitting and listening to government proceedings from *"fossil dicks"* in the United States government, men in their octogenarian years who are spending more money on the military marching band than they are on alternative sources of energy. Violet prays for the souls of the unwashed politicians who walk the crooked mile and for the corrupt environment.

Have you ever paused to look at the overflowing abundance of nature? In this way of prosperity thinking, the pail is half-full. Mercedes got her pail of milk. The lesson here; the prosperity principle, opposite of the scarcity principle. To those living under the prosperity principle comes abundance and learning that we cannot fail, where barriers become challenges seen as positive opportunities to grow, and we bless them accordingly. To those living under the scarcity principle, the pail is half-empty in their negative way of thinking, and there is never enough milk money. "Bless this pail of milk," Mercedes thanks God and the heifer.

There is no set stage in a woman's life when she becomes wild and independent. "Free-reining" is up to her — what she can handle, the load she can carry, and how she copes with herself determines the great turning point in life.

She has to make tracks all of her own when the time comes, and sometimes it requires behavior society deems "unbecoming" to women who have been expected to display only their softness.

Sadie and Vi know what stage they are in and they don't back off from it one snaffle "bit" in the horse's mouth. This part comes for which there is no preparation and it comes today.

It is one thing to move wild horses from South Dakota to a bucking horse auction, but is entirely another to happen upon a herd of wild horses on your own property, and seize a chance-in-a-lifetime to live out a day in the life of a mustang runner.

"My God!" Vi gasps. Her finger pulls downward like a water-witching fork. "Cowgirl, do you know what those are?" Vi points down into the boxed canyon.

"Wild mustangs!" Sadie snaps.

"I can't imagine heaven without them," Vi says, with big tears in her eyes. Most people will never see them in a lifetime, but Vi has seen them twice now, once before in the Rocky Mountains of Lincoln, Montana in an almost identical setting in a boxed canyon in Helena National Forest, both times a happenstance and both times emotional.

"Me neither," Sadie answers. "Makes you want to try harder to get there."

Thought alone isn't enough. To make it work, they are going to have to throw in all of their combined power and then some. They are sitting on a keg of dynamite atop their horses and things will never be the same once they light the match.

The herds of wild horses today that roam the western deserts of the United States are descendents of domesticated animals that escaped and turned feral. The modern horse appeared two million years ago, evolving as the forests dwindled and the grasslands spread, creating a longer-legged animal capable of rapid speed.

Converting from Mormonism to *Dreamtime* doesn't change the horse, nor does it change the definition of wild or domestic, and it most certainly doesn't change the name of religion. Sadie and Vi don't choose labels, but they choose language carefully when defining who they are and what they believe.

Christian teaching regards the horse as representing the swift passage of life. In Australia, galloping free over the arid rangeland are wild horses known as brumbies, as many as 600,000 making up the world's largest herd.

Catering to spiritual seekers, modern-day religions are dropping labels so as to not put their followers into a box theologically.

The Mormon Church now wants to be called by its full and original, proper name given by revelation to church founder Joseph Smith in 1838 – the Church of Jesus Christ of Latter-day Saints. They want those to know they are part of the Christian family, trying to silence the critics who view Mormonism as a cult, a new religious tradition incompatible with Christianity because of its unorthodox beliefs, namely polygamy. The Church distances itself from modern-day polygamists and any LDS member caught in polygamy are excommunicated.

Even the atheists want to now be called "Freethinkers" and there is a debate among some Quakers about whether they should encourage use of "Friends," their former name. Few still call the Pentecostals "Holy Rollers," an insulting term coined by opponents of the movement. When it comes to how the public perceives a religion, obviously names matter. Think of this next time you pin a name tag on at a function which requires you to label yourself; a case in point about the power of a name.

On a scale of blue-ribbon, Vi places the mustangs superior to humans. There may not have been a more spiritual scene in the world. If there was water here, trucks would be here, not these magnificent animals. Vi knows how to work it, the government red tape. She'll apply for the wild horse permits later. "Let's claim 'em!" Vi lets out a rebel yell followed by "Haw, haw, rawhide!"

They take off, rumbling into the canyon, lighting the stick of TNT, throwing the coil of feminist fuse and caution to the wind. From here on out, things get pretty western. Sadie and Vi are screwed down on those Ozark Rancher's Basketweave saddles as tight as a "Morgan" silver dollar on a frontier store counter, not easily plucked down in those days.

There is no hand-tooled saddle for an award; this is no pony-express type horse race, but if they are lucky and still alive, the finish line is in their corral.

Balance and coordination combined with timing leaves no room for inaccuracies. Dust is an evil and so is the pheasants they are flushing out — or worst yet — if one of the pheasants collides with horse or rider at this great speed, it could be a disaster.

Neither Sadie nor Vi is looking to have a transitional wreck at forty. The tragedy of a wreck would be that they are so exclusively and spiritually oriented in the onset of midlife. They have made the transitional move from the biological sphere to the cultural sphere and converted from Mormonism to *Dreamtime.*

Sadie and Vi have a world full of good instincts and a Marlboro spirit and that is what is going to bring these wild mustangs in. Instead of driving them straight once they pull out of the canyon, they drive them at an angle, Sadie up front along beside them and Vi running a hundred yards back from Monday to Sunday, one for every day of the week, seven of the most beautiful wild mustangs you have ever seen.

Every few seconds, the thirty-six crescent-moon hoofs plow up the buffalo grass, hurling the divots, not exempt from uprooting, but only in this special case. Created by the hand of God, or by *Dreamtime* ancestors, whatever our religious beliefs, we must try to keep the land as we find it, but occasionally we disturb it for the good. Bringing in the wild mustangs is a spiritual happenstance for Sadie and Vi, knowing many species can sue them for nature violation and for creating an unattractive nuisance.

Sagebrush Rebellion takes over, but Vi and Sadie have not violated their contract with the Sky Heroes, the Creators who first shaped the land in Australian Aboriginal myth, *Dreamtime.* Like the Aboriginals, Sadie and Vi regard this land with the greatest respect. It is the root of their religion and sacred law.

Dreamtime was long ago, before time itself, when mythological ancestors and supernaturals traveled across featureless lands, stopping to dig yams, hunt kangaroos, spear a goose, or toss the bones of a fish. Wherever the ancestors stopped, the landscape changed; a waterhole appeared or perhaps a rock formation grew, each becoming a sacred site where clans were born, where they lived in bush camps, and then the missionaries came.

Changing gears, Sadie spurs her horse, thinking ahead what they are going to do once they get to the corral. She is sure the gate is closed and these mustangs aren't going to wait around. Vi knows what Sadie is thinking. She is thinking the same thing herself, but they aren't within talking distance. Sadie throws her right hand up, the same one she used to throw her half of the coil of feminist fuse, and points ahead, meaning it is all up to Vi to bring the mustangs in. They are only about a half-mile out and running at the speed they are, it will only take but a wild, eight-second ride to get to the finish line.

Tailgating the "hung" outlaw one with his penis extended, Vi shoots past him, getting a lick of sperm flying in the air when he ejaculates from being damn excited. She'll put his dick in the dirt if she has to! She has a coil of feminist fuse to spare. "Save it, Outlaw — you'll need it one day!" she hollers, her throat hoarse and dry from the dust. She wipes her lips off and cracks them in a conspiratorial grin. Reeling it in, he may or may not have heard her next comment, blowing him off with, *"I'm a gay woman, so don't waste that big one on me!"*

Sadie pounds a few nails quickly, securing loose boards. She doesn't know what to expect. She is choking from the dust of *Sagebrush Rebellion* and her nostrils flare to the overpowering sweetness of horse lather. Her partner is out there about to make a very satisfying end to this serendipitous day. Hospitably, Sadie cleaves a bale of timothy hay and stands by respectfully, taking her western hat off like you do at a rodeo before the *National Anthem*. She gets goose bumps and teary-eyed just like you do at the event just described.

By the time it is all over, they look like a street-cleaner's broom, dirty and frazzled. "What the hell did we just do?" Sadie asks.

In her polished speech and confident manner, Vi answers as if she is putting her name to a maverick bill. "The ink goes down dark, bold, and cranky, hon, but as it dries, the letters evaporate leaving behind tame gray shapes." Ridden hard and put up wet, the metaphor is yet to be proven, but it will be. Somewhere in between the lick of stallion sperm and taste of mare snot hurled at her, Vi knows what her method of taming will be, and she discusses it with Sadie and because of the day's soul-stirring emotionalism and link with *Dreamtime*, they go to bed passionately attached. You often find them this way. In each of us, there is a dreamer, and a rebel, where sex and religion ride together.

Mercedes Cade has grown fond of Violet Mace-Reese. That's not *all* there is to it. Mercedes Cade has fallen in love with Violet Mace-Reese. But, she doesn't want to be dependent on this emotion or feel guilty with what religion may have to do with all of it or give her power away, handing out fistfuls of energy, sexual, creative, or otherwise. *Can a woman not genetically trained as a lesbian learn the creative process of making love to another woman without guilt and — which asks another question — without dependency?*

Let's use the falcon to try to find the answers. Say a woman we know — the *Lace Falconer* — uses the falcon, trains it all the while illustrating the act of dependency. Living its life out as a figment of powerlessness, operating from dependency, the trained falcon — after making a small game kill — always returns the prey to the *Lace Falconer* of which the *Lace Falconer* offers the falcon a small chunk of the kill as a reward. Notice that the *Lace Falconer* has trained dependency into the falcon until the falcon forgets freedom, and the source of the falcon's food is associated only with the *Lace Falconer*. The answer lies in this. When we become dependent, we forget we are our own source of food and give away power to the ones we feel are superior to us. It proves it through falconry. The falcon would have taken the prey all for itself if this were not true.

Mercedes sees admirable affection in Violet because she sees these same characteristics in herself. She can't allow herself to see in terms of superior or inferior, but to see through reflection what she admires in herself. Ironically, by coming to the convent, she has not only found her set-point through missionary work — very good — but at the same time, she has come into both religious guilt and sexual guilt created here at the convent — not so very good, a downside to her eighteen-month commitment.

Organized religion is often used to produce guilt and manipulate behavior. Church-related guilt is based somehow on letting God down, giving one the message to feel ashamed with "if you loved God, you wouldn't behave this way," and "You've disobeyed God's rules. You should be ashamed of yourself."

Sexual guilt goes hand-in-hand with religious guilt. Probably the biggest place in society where a woman's guilt flourishes is in the realm of sex. Sexual fantasies about Violet are a guilt center for Mercedes, located in her cunt. (Can she say *cunt*? Well, probably not in this environment. *Re-enter* this one: Sexual fantasies about Violet are a guilt center for Mercedes located *"where morning glories twine around the door."*)

God forbid she should masturbate when she is feeling overpowered by her sexual desire. "You must not," Sister Pish said at orientation. "Masturbation leads to greater fantasy and loneliness. Pray instead, asking the Lord to understand what you are going through and for guidance to help you to accept and understand your sexuality. A proper way to relieve your biological sexual tension is to get involved in volunteer work. Channel your passions into God's service, helping people in his kingdom. Get involved in the Lord's recreation."

Mercedes and Violet volunteer at the soup kitchen, their charitable choice. Mormon missionaries are required to perform eight hours of volunteer work weekly. Serving meals to the hungry is the compassionate way of the missionary, talking God, putting hope in people's hearts — namely the homeless — but it does nothing to ease Mercedes' sexual hunger. What to do? Sister Pish says it is wrong to keep feeding one's mind with salacious thoughts through any medium, *especially* masturbation.

Mercedes tries substitutes for masturbation. The versatile jujube often substitutes for apples, pears, plums, or figs in recipes. Some days, she goes to the jujube trees for consolation. The fruit from the jujube tree cures so many problems; from sore throat, fever, and sweet tooth to what-to-give-for-Christmas, so Mercedes employs them as "chastity apples" to avert lesbian lust.

Just like masturbation, the jujube was unpopular for many years because processing involves so much work. The skin is tough and it takes Mercedes time to peel each one. Through peeling the jujubes, Mercedes is trying to learn how to discipline her sexual desire. Lately, the jujubes are enjoying a rebirth of popularity. Perhaps masturbation is *"coming"* into a similar rebirth of popularity. Mercedes wants to give herself goose bumps of shivery pleasure. She wants to choose orgasm for herself and not be told she "must not." But as long as she is here, she is going to honor Sister Pish's "must-nots" and the tenets of the Mormon faith.

How many ways can you "ring your bell?" You can pluck it. You can hit it. You can shake it. You can thump it! It is an *easy* instrument to play. You have to have a lot of hand-eye coordination. To keep her fingers away from her crotch, Violet busies her hands with handbells, her substitute for masturbation.

She is a member of Sister Pish's Missionary Handbell Choir. They play inspirational songs including "Lord, I Lift Your Name," "Simple Gifts," and "Beautiful Savior."

A handbell concert is a rare treat. Ringers line up in front of their tables in an auditorium, while the audience sits in the balcony looking down at the performance.

The handbells are placed in front of the ringers on special padding. The ringers wait without motion with bells in hand until it is their turn to ring. You can only ring your bells. Some ringers who play the smaller, higher-note bells play up to eight bells in a piece. If a ringer makes a mistake, it is undeniable. Unlike playing in a symphony, where a mistake may be covered by the other instruments, if a ringer misses a cue, there is a small hole of silence where ringers follow the creed: better *never* than late.

Those who play the middle notes are usually the busiest ringers, having an average of four bells, two natural notes, a sharp, and a flat. Violet is a big-bell ringer, only having two bells, her ringing sparse. She likes things in increments of two; the handbells being no different.

Handbell ringing isn't one of the Lord's cheapest recreations. Depending on their size, handbells cost from $100 to $350. Most buy their bells by the octave, a group of eight octaves, which cost about $2,000. Serious ringers start with two or three octaves and add on.

Big bells weigh over twelve pounds and are rung by using two hands. Ringers wear special gloves with tread on them for a better grip, to keep from getting blisters, and to protect the finish on the pricey brass bells.

There are many pieces written specially for handbell choirs. The music resembles piano music, but with more notes in the chords. Symbols and abbreviations tell players what to do with the bell if it is other than ringing. They can thumb damp, meaning thumping the bell; mart lift, which is hitting the bell on the padded table and lifting to ring in the air, or the bell can be lightly hit with a mallet. There are so many ways to play a bell as there are to play with yourself, or *masturbate: "Where morning glories twine around the door!"*

Pluck it! Hit it! Shake it! THUMP IT!

Inspired by the labyrinth, Vi's popular memory blueprints the secret to taming the mustangs. She lays the ink on drafting paper where it goes down dark and bold flowing from the slit in the tip of the quill, the concentric circle evaporating as it dries, leaving behind a tame gray shape.

Has it ever been used before? Vi hasn't heard of using the concept of the labyrinth to tame a horse, but she is going to build one. The value of her equestrian labyrinth, the concentric circle she laid down in ink as a training aid is obvious to her.

The labyrinth has also been interpreted as a spiritual focal point where the walkers are drawn to the center where eye to eye meet in meditational territory. By the end of the journey, one arrives in tameness and gentle spirit.

Now this makes sense to Vi. A horse's vision makes a big difference in how successful you are in training it. It is all in the focal point; retina, optic nerve, and lens. Eye placement has a great deal to do with the horse's ability to do the job. To properly train the mustangs, Vi is going to have to see things from their view.

The equine eye does not focus the same way as ours. The horse's lens doesn't adjust for distances. A horse's vision depends on head carriage. In order to see close objects, the horse has to lower its head so that the light passes through the lens and strikes the upper portion of the retina. To see at a distance, the horse has to rotate its eyes forward and raise its head, causing the light to strike the lower portion of the retina. A frontal blind spot is caused by eye placement because the eyes are at the side of the horse's head and the rear blind spot results in the horse's inability to see around its rump.

Modern-day horses evolved from an ancestor who had to be alert for predators, keeping their head down for long periods where they needed a visual field that would expose the area around and behind it. This is why the eyes evolved to the side of the horse's head.

The Great Horse-maker built the equine in a very unusual way, in that the eye rotating muscles are connected to the ears. When a horse pricks its ears forward, it is also rotating its eyes to the front. When a horse has its ears laid back, it can't possibly see in front.

Horses with eyes more to the front make better jumpers. A horse with a broad forehead and wide, intelligent eyes make a better mount. Horses with small, poorly-shaped eyes have bad tempers because of poor rearward vision.

Vi studies each of the mustangs' eyes, clearly meeting head on with each individual's eyes to understand mental attitude, noting the relationship between the ears and eyes. Remember when Vi told the stallion – "Save it, Outlaw – you'll need it one day" – referring to his ejaculation of *Sagebrush Rebellion* sperm, then him reeling it in, she wonders if he heard her comment? He may not have. His cropped ears indicate he was a winter colt who lost the tips of his ears to frostbite. This could be a challenge in that perhaps he has no natural vision problems, but he may be creating them simply from lack of attention and concentration from impaired hearing, thus not being able to carry his head where it belongs and his ears would always be back.

The stallion is a symbol of sexuality. The taming of a stallion implies the taming of sexuality, which fits like a tight pair of jeans tonight. There is nothing that can tame Sadie's sexuality, except for her stuck zipper. Vi brings out the zipper wax stick and rubs it up and down the metal teeth, plays with the idea for a bit. "How's that feel?" she asks, minding Sadie's beeswax.

"Like a dyke queen bee with a brass stinger and I need it bad, Montana," Sadie answers.

Montana rubs the wax stick right into *Dreamtime* where Australia has giant bumblebees. She gets Down Under on her knees and buzzes her lips over Sadie's zipper, buzzing syllables, varying the sound by moving her tongue around like the way you do when you play a didgeridoo, an Australian instrument made from a termite-hollowed eucalyptus branch used in spiritual ceremonies, the low drone used for relaxation and meditation. *"How bad?"*

The knowers of the female soul practice disciplines to keep the deeper levels constantly in reach. It may be physical work, intellectual work, or spiritual work, or sometimes a combination of all three.

The modern-day quest for spiritual solace is in accord with the serenity-seeking woman. Spirituality is gaining popularity over "religion." It isn't that spirituality is pushing out religion. Spirituality is *shaking up* religion. Spirituality embraces a wider body of experiences, and is a matter of the woman being open to new things, experimenting with spiritual resources other than the doctrines of the church they have inherited from their parents.

Prayer and worship are considered spiritual by most women, those same women also using "spiritual" to describe a walk in the woods. Modern day feminists and lesbians consider sex to be the ultimate spiritual experience.

Violet Mace-Reese will be remembered as a rebel politician/environmentalist. She is finished with politics and she is saying it here at the Pish Convent where she discovered her appreciation of spirituality has far more value than her political career. Like Mercedes, Violet has no intention of making this her life's work. It is just too structured of an environment to live by all throughout life for the personalities of these two women. Violet is comfortable in "going against the tide."

Violet and Mercedes have been set free to serve. Being here at the convent is a positive, liberating experience. Too often, others see faith as just a set of rules which takes the joy out of life. Nothing can be farther from the truth here.

In today's society, we are losing the art of serving. Service is rapidly becoming extinct. Gas stations, discount stores, and supermarkets are increasingly becoming more self-service. If you want something nowadays, most likely you have to get it yourself.

As Christians, the S/sisters at the Pish Convent have been called upon to serve others. In a lengthy, animated sermon not likely to be forgotten, Sister Pish's words echo off the walls of the Church of Pish. "On Judgment Day, the question will not be how much have you got, but how much have you given? Not how much have you won, but how much have you done?"

Hallelujah! For Christ's sake! Oops...where morning glories twine around the door. The winning sermon bounces around like numbered air-blown ping-pong lottery balls, and the winning numbers for sixteen months ago for fifteen million dollars were 5-6-14-29-30-31. Those were the numbers Mercedes Cade picked. You heard it right; Mercedes is a millionaire many times over!

Prosperity has had only one meaning for too long — money. And Mercedes knows it. Again, the peaks of happiness — being swept off your feet, climbing "fourteeners," or winning the lottery are all nice, but happiness comes down to being serenely content on an even level, finding a set-point.

There are those who have treated money as a savior. Well guess what, it's not! Too many of these thinkers speak of income in the same breath as *their* value, usually those with a low self-image.

Contrary to popular belief, money is *not* the root of all evil. Like everything else, it is neither good nor bad, nor moral nor immoral. The moral issue is in the *intention* of the user. Money can be used to promote life and love, or it can be used to destroy life and love in many different ways.

Money should be thought of in holistic terms, prospering naturally, using a holistic approach to controlling how it will be spent, appreciating the good it can do. Money has no power in itself, but controlling how we spend it gives *us* power.

If we are going to ask for power in great amounts, then we had better be prepared to handle it. An example of what happens when we are unprepared for the power of money comes through the study of million-dollar lottery winners. The vast majority are usually broke within five years. This says they have not developed a holistic approach where they could benefit from their windfall for very long, letting money control them instead of them being in control of their money.

Mercedes came to the Pish Convent to learn how to become friends with her money. She came with two questions: How do you want to help others with your money and what do you want to have achieved with your money when you leave this plane of life?

Money doesn't belong hoarded. Receiving depends greatly upon giving, and when done in the right spirit, our return is increased many times over.

She hasn't told anyone of her lottery sweepstakes, not even her mother, and she intends to keep it that way for a while. Her honest, hard work here is reward within itself. Mindful of her several Colorado bank accounts, most importantly; she takes in account her spiritual prosperity and banks it heavily in Zion, the promised land.

Readying herself for lights out at 10:30 PM, Mercedes is peeling her last "chastity apple" for the evening, reading biblical passages propped open on her bedside table: *"knock, and the door shall be opened unto you."* Just about that time (and how serendipitous it is), there is a soft knock on her cottage door.

"Who is it?" she asks her voice softer at this hour.

"Violet."

Oh! This is a big "must-not." The wind, the rain, the pollen — anything but the *door!*

"Keeping mattress tags on for years because they say *do not* remove under *penalty* of law," Mercedes answers, clutching a jujube so tight the whites of her knuckles show the strength of "chastity apples."

Violet laughs so hard from the other side of the door; she falls to the obedient ground. She cuts the damn tags off, making a case here for being a social rebel. She is a shrugger, resisting enculturation and meaningless policies.

"You don't *really* keep mattress and furniture tags on all those years, do you?" Violet asks.

"Yes. You know I can't open this door for you," Mercedes answers, still clutching the jujube and whispering under her breath, *"God's little green apples."*

"Yes," Violet laughs. "I got what I came for."

"What was that?" Mercedes asks.

"Testing your faith. Attraction lurks here — the folly of must-nots." Violet goes back to her cottage to "ring her bell." There is no point in rebelling just for the sake of rebelling, but there are nice rewards in being your own person.

He tells the story and his wife confirms his words. Moses Piltershmitz, his wife Zea, (pronounced Zay-ah) and their teenage son, Jediah, are Mennonites traveling through Clovis by draft horses and carriage.

"This very same coach was used to carry mail and passengers from Fort Bragg, California to Cloverdale, California. This coach was later then sold to Wells Fargo," Moses tells, transporting their imaginations back to the Old West in the days of high-button shoes and the two-cent stamp.

"Moses tells it right," Zea interjects.

"Devil's mark," Moses points to the bullet hole in the side of the coach. Although the little circular hole is neat, this slight imperfection marred the side of the nineteenth century coach, which was the victim of an armed robbery by bandits unknown.

His Amish brothers have buggy factories in Pennsylvania, one of their incomes coming from the three R's of carriage work — repairing, restoring, and replicating — their religious sect whose beliefs requires members to reject "worldly things."

Moses operates a school for carriage driving where old-style horse-drawn coaches are making a comeback as tourist attractions and driving competitions. "Our basic need is to have our coach's seat upholstered in new hide — full-grain kip if you've got it," Moses says, hoping Sadie and Vi can fill his order.

From The Convent To The Rawhide

"Papa Moses tells it right," seventeen-year-old Jediah says, tipping his black pilgrim hat, extending his hand out to shake. What a gentleman he is, and a looker, with shoulder-length brown hair and kind, thoughtful blue eyes.

"Respectfully, I'm taking my wheelwright apprenticeship on a small farm west of here. We got into the coach business after harvesting corn by hand behind a rickety wagon in bad need of repair," Jediah explains. "Strong wheelwright skills are the crux of a good carriage shop."

"Jediah tells it right. We have no proper amount of upholstery knowledge," Moses says.

"We can help reverse this generation of deterioration," Vi says, keeping with Mennonite speak.

"Most of the time, they roll in under their own power," Sadie says, "and sometimes the carriages fall apart after we push them a bit."

"Take away the power lines and the blacktopped country roads, my good Lord," Moses bows his head.

"Papa Moses tells it right," Jediah speaks, then he spiels off carriage-ride etiquette the Omaha Herald published in 1877. "Don't discuss politics or religion. Don't swear. If you have anything to drink in a bottle with a label, pass it around," he pauses for a moment, and reaches for a fresh bottle of whiskey under the seat in the coach. He breaks the seal and twists off the cap and pours himself a cap full, making sure his lips don't touch the bottle keeping in the good graces of etiquette, then passes the bottle to Sadie who takes the first pull from the bottle.

"Thank you, you handsome soul," Sadie says.

"Jediah tells it right," Moses says when the bottle comes to him. "Continue, my son."

"Don't point out where there have been murders committed, especially if there are women and children passengers. Don't smoke a strong pipe inside the coach. Don't spit on the leeward side. If the team runs away, sit still and take our chances. Don't grease your hair; travel is dusty. The best seat in the coach is the one next to the driver — you get less jolts."

"Amen," Zea offers, giving Moses a tender side hug around his waist.

Sadie and Vi go through the stack of hides and pull out a fine one that measures about seventeen square feet.

"Here's a kip," Vi says. A kip is the skin of a large calf. "Full grain is all we grow here. It appears just the way it is taken off the animal. Only the hair has been removed and the grain is left on. We don't fence or brand. You'll see no scars. Full grain is different from top grain. Top grain hide is often sanded to remove scars and then sprayed to cover up the work. Our hides are processed at the tannery where the size is measured with as little waste as possible," Vi explains.

"She tells it right," Sadie says. "Leather is measured in ounces. One ounce equals 1/64" in thickness. Heavier leathers come from the hides of mature animals."

"That figures out to $170 at seventeen square feet, at $10 per square foot for black-dyed kip plus $25 an hour for labor and $12 for buttons," Vi quotes.

"We will pay the price. How long will it take to give new life to the seat?" Moses inquires.

"We can have it finished in three hours. The quality will be high right down to covering and setting the buttons," Sadie answers.

Jediah unbolts the seat and hauls it down. "Do you mind if we watch your skill? I'm a quick study," he says, "a short-courser apprentice." He is soft-spoken, but keep in mind that he has grown up quick for some reason, keeping his emotions to himself.

"Ask a thousand questions if you like. You're welcome to see us work. We're proud of what we grow," Sadie and Vi both say. They like this family who seem to *like* each other.

From The Convent To The Rawhide

Sadie waxes the black linen thread by running it over her puck of beeswax until Jediah decides he might like to try. "Why do you do this?" he asks.

"Waxing the thread reduces tangles and prevents fraying," Vi answers. "It lengthens the thread's life so the stitches don't come undone." She shows him how to make a proper paper pattern of the seat to use as a measuring guide to cut the exact size of the leather with no waste.

After the leather is cut, Sadie rolls the overstitch wheel along the leather to mark the spacing for smooth, even stitches. "Seven stitches per inch we'll go with," she says, and threads an S-curved needle with a chisel point.

Vi cuts a sheet of quarter-inch seating foam and uses the same paper pattern, then goes for the Spanish moss for stuffing. She winks at Sadie, teasing her with the salty memory of the harvest at Muleshoe. It is tucker (food) for thought.

"You two women work as friendly as this team of horses who always travel in pairs and are always in earshot of each other. Where did you take your sisterly training?" Jediah inquires. He doesn't care which one answers, so Sadie does.

"From the convent to the rawhide, self-trained, from then on, by books and products from the Tandy Leather Company. We're former Mormon missionaries having served in St. George, Utah at the Pish Convent."

Jediah stays quiet for a moment, just the way he does when he takes the coach over hills, around bends, across creeks, and through willows thinking independently, taking it all in. His carefully chosen words are strong enough that he can carry on no matter what. "You can successfully raise horses without white rail fences and you can build coaches without a single piece of mechanized equipment, but the two things you cannot do without are God and knowledge." *Well said!* Although his parents don't hear the comment, they are probably the ones who instilled Jediah with this prosperous way of thinking. Moses and Zea are taking a nap in the back of the coach.

Using only the simplest hand tools and no tool that has resulted from technology in the last fifty years, Sadie and Vi proudly display their old-day tools, including awls, chisels, groovers, hammers, saws, planers, axes, hatchets, whetstones, knives, and anvils. "Our furniture is only made from hand tools, no power tools. We only use reclaimed wood that we salvage from old barns and what rustic material we find that has a rebel personality," Vi says.

"Now that needs some explaining," Jediah says, "How in God's name is personality borne into a stick of wood?" he asks.

"Its unique personality just rubs off on you, marked by youth at one time, kind of like your personality has rubbed off on us," Vi compliments. "See this simple piece of furniture? It's a stitching horse we made. Whichever one of us will straddle it and sit down on the oblong bench seat curved to fit a woman's anatomy comfortably, narrower between where our thighs part, then we clamp our small item in the jaw where we have a food-controlled tension arm, making it easy to stitch and lace leather."

"What would you think if Vi told you about where we found the wood to make the stitching horse, and what old-day activities went on there?" Sadie asks, testing his level of religious obedience, but if he drinks whiskey...

"Would it be a particular spot that yielded a dozen garters and deep canyons smelling of rosewater?" he asks. "I've heard many Mennonite sermons — some of them damn right historical."

Vi laughs as hard as she did at the convent when she knocked on Mercedes Cade's cottage door when Mercedes used the analogy of removing the mattress tag as opening the door, the key words, *do not* and *penalty*. At times, religion does lend humor in an appropriate way, but you have to keep your ears open because it isn't too often God allows bawdy humor. One day back at the convent, when one of the elder Sisters accidentally blew Sister Pish's dress up with the gas-powered leaf blower when she got too close. "Damn inventions!" Sister Pish cursed. *Oops!* "Where morning glories twine around the door."

"With permission from the straight-laced owner of a ghost town that was once in a silver-bearing zone, the owner wanted the ghosts of gaudy ladies in this town's house of ill-repute removed," Vi began, "so Sadie and I seized the opportunity to honor the owner's request, and because the giant of a storyteller that Sadie Cade is, I'll let her put new paint on old boards and tell you the story, Jediah."

"With no monetary lust for the decorator's market, we negotiated for the old boards, or *old broads*," Sadie widely pronounces for effect. She is prepared to put the flesh back on the wooden remains, bringing back the oldest profession in the world.

Whether he is truly rehearsing his virginity or wants to ride the stitching horse for historical interest, Jediah asks, "Do you mind?"

"Throw your leg over the old girls," Sadie says, assigning herself "Madam," giving him permission for a "feel" of old-day lust. "She is our finest piece."

"The thrill of exploration is still here and so is temptation in the untamed town in which the obstinate whiskey dealer set up shop. Don't try and take your conventional car, though. The coach will do just fine following the Rosewater Trail," Jediah imagines, his thoughts on how the trip might be back then on the stage route to the garters and rosewater cleavage. "Old towns were four to ten miles apart, close enough to reach the saloons and these ladies of the evening by coach — until the makers of the Model T put the buggy whips out of business. In came Henry Ford and cheap asphalt, connecting towns ten, twenty, even thirty miles apart. The dust was reduced, but the lust was not. The land was settled by homesteaders and dryland farmers. In came the Homestead Act and with it came back the dust from discing crosswind. There was too much land plowed that would have been better left in grass. The whiskey was swilled to wash down the dust, the whores bought to satisfy the rise brought on by the whiskey," Jediah sermonizes. "One thing leads to another."

Modern-day ministry can be found in tattoo parlors, piercing studios, and punk-rock concerts. Jediah finds his ministry in the carriage factory on a farm west of here where his unorthodox ministry complements his wheelwright apprenticeship. While setting steel rims on wagon wheels and operating a wire stretcher, spoke pointer, and tendon cutter, he spiels what history he knows and applies it to religion. "I'm not about promoting God," Jediah says, "I'm about attracting youth to country life through the philosophy of religion, finding my converts in the Lord's wheel, saying to them, 'your grandkids will be driving this one day and God will be at the reins.' You can bet your tintype we learn by doing, especially repairing and restoring the days of old. Those who choose an expression of faith rather than inheriting one given to them are more apt to follow it with greater commitment. I'm confident my words are understood when my converts can supervise and see that I maintain quality control, unlike an assembly-line operation where buyers should avoid cars put out on Fridays and Mondays."

"Who does a young man like you learn such an arcane trade from?" Vi asks.

Jediah smiles and seems somewhat taken aback by the sincerity of the question. "By doing it with an Amish master wheelwright peering over my shoulder."

Sadie continues the story. "Black widow spiders crawling underneath the old boards ..." then Jediah interjects.

"Now there's a sermon," he says. "The black widow mates and then she kills. The ones before us who spent their coins

From The Convent To The Rawhide

for this one with pretty poison; those early years were boom times with which great miserliness came from such places. One has to be aware of the history of these locations and apply it to modern-day religion. Who built the churches? Why was the town developed? Who had money? What caused the town to boom and most important, what caused the boom to collapse and the town to die? After telling people this, though, they will have to play with her, the black widow, at least once, and a few will give up in disgust, pain, maybe death, and empty pocketbooks."

Sadie finishes the story. "We found amongst the widows under the porch, some wheat-straws (pennies) and a cache of private mint-issue Mormon coins. It has been said; 'often coins show up where a bad crack is.'" How it is meant is however one wants to take it, but how else can you take it being where it is? As for the Mormon coins, they were spiritually circulated until they got into the wrong hands, most likely circulated on the Mormon Trail in 1847 leading out of Iowa to Zion.

Moses in the back, Zea up front with Jediah at the reins, roll onto their promised land where the high summer oats wave in the breeze where a coach runs through it, perhaps a scene Robert Redford might approve of for a movie.

Walking to the mailbox is a beautiful experience for Sister Pish. A woman of seventy, she says, "You're never too old to walk to the mailbox." The towheaded prankster neighbor boy has put straw in her mailbox again. "Where morning glories twine around the door!"

She takes the letters into the Church of Pish and sits down on the pews covered with red cushions that match the red carpet in the aisles. There is always a Mason jar of water sitting on the pulpit for when her throat goes dry during her lengthy sermons. She passes out handheld paper fans with printed advertisements on the back that serve for air-conditioning.

She sorts out the letters addressed to the S/sisters from their loved ones and pulls out her personal mail — utility bills, liability insurance premiums, reservations, and inquiries from potential missionaries. A special light spotlights one piece of her mail. The halo of golden light falls upon the envelope, coming from the stained glass window facing west. The window is a signature garden picture of the jujube fruit trees and a cross. She puts the envelope beside her on the pew, watching the prism of light highlight the radiance of whatever is sealed inside.

"Remember this," Sister Pish said at one of the first sermons Mercedes heard her give. "Whoever sows sparingly will reap sparingly, and whoever sows generously will also reap generously. God loves a cheerful giver."

The letters

A true friend is the person who steps in when the whole world steps out. You have enriched my life and allowed me to find the better part of me. The colors hold us together through crisis and circumstance. You reached in and put a tube of blue neon around my heart.

There's a neighbor with whom you share a glass of wine from upscale goblets, commemorating the simplicities of living on good terms with one another; the one who lends a hand to put up a curtain rod or mows your lawn while you are away. It is nice just knowing you are across the road.

A lover listens and writes what is shorthand what the heart dictates. It's the most intimate thing you can be to another. Comparable to the flame in the tealight or the facet cut in the bead, the lover compliments the other. Simply, a lover is the cross-stitch in pillow talk and the warmth in the blanket.

As a mentor/protégé, we have gone through something similar and helped each other through it, perhaps without even knowing it. We share a passion for the written word and are bent on living life as an art form. Mentors don't have to reintroduce themselves after years of absence. It is timeless and ageless and positive.

It doesn't matter who the letters are addressed to. There are four sister missionaries who received letters today. One is from a friend, one from a neighbor, one from a lover, and one from a mentor. The above lines are abridged, keeping in mind most of the lower-case sister missionaries are not here because of their testimonies or beliefs, but while here, they are all strictly adhering to the tenets of the Mormon faith. Most are here to find the better part of themselves.

Sent by a sentimental gushing guardian angel closer than you'd think, Sister Pish has taken back to the Church of Pish the unopened piece of mail the special light had spotlighted by the sun coming through the stained glass window earlier in the day.

She sits the envelope in the same spot on the pew beside her this evening; this time, a halo of blue-green light backlit by the moon comes through the stained glass window, the color of any Eden worth the name, then ...

Sister Pish is reckoning with an evil force. There comes a devastating loss of the higher thought process and a weakened sense of the power of prayer. Sister Pish bows her head.

"A person should always live," the Church of Pish instructs, "as if the end of days and the Last Judgment could arrive tomorrow."

Troubling signs, memory lapse, confusion, and erroneous perceptions of reality, what we know today as Alzheimer's, the black dungeon of hell. With terror and panic in her eyes, she silently weeps.

"Hale-Bopp, grab that envelope!" the devil rips. "The comet has appeared." He is dressed in disguise as a greedy churchman like the ones who encourage millennial fears deliberately so people will give their material possessions to the church. Apocryphal stories are told of the world at its end, devised from the devil's inflamed mind. "Hand it over, Sister. The Lord Almighty is calling you in. You've lost your mind: the end is near. He can have your soul in trade for the envelope," the devil says.

Flipped out of her God-loving mind, Sister Pish goes up to the podium where her wet Mason jar is. "Cleanse your soul, devil," she hallucinates, tossing the water out of the jar, then reaches inside the pulpit, pulling a bottle of jujube cough syrup from the shelf, thinking she is pouring the devil a hellish picnic of decadence — an alcoholic beverage he thrives on and tempts the weak with. Alcohol abuse is at an all-time high, leveling off from time to time with the techniques and disciplines of Alcoholics Anonymous, including making amends, honest disclosure, making sacrifices, fasting, keeping silence, pilgrimages, reciting mantras, doing penance, and keeping the devil at bay.

His blubbery lips quiver and his forked tongue wallows in the dirty creases where it curls at the corner of his mouth, just a horrid sight, drooling foul-smelling saliva caused from cirrhosis onto his singed, red goatee. "Go on, take it, you SON OF A BITCH!" Sister Pish curses; Alzheimer's impairs language, behavior, judgment, movement, coordination, and causes personality changes.

She fills twenty-six Mason jars tuned with spring water. Most don't know it, but Mozart wrote for glass harmonica, a set of drinking glasses partially filled with water that produced sounds by rubbing the glass rims with a wet finger. Donizetti wrote his famous "Mad Scene" in "Lucifer" with glass harmonica in mind, but when no glass harmonica player could be found for the Naples premiere, he had to restore the duet for flute and soprano.

Considered her "Mad Scene" in "Lucifer," Sister Pish plays the glass harmonica in wild syncopation, the devil's computer downloading a musical instrument boneyard containing instrument relics that have fallen into disuse — including the glass harp, the arpeggione (invented in Vienna in 1823), the baryton (an eighteenth century predecessor of the cello), the ophicleide (displaced by the tuba when invented in Paris in the 1880s), the Theremin (the first electronic instrument invented by a Russian in 1920), and the devil's favorite – the serpent (a bass woodwind, precursor of the ophicleide, which is the French word for "serpent with keys," created around 1600 and shaped like a snake).

It is a showdown. "Those canning jars won't play a tune, you wrinkled old nun. The rim is too thick. You need the fine rims of Austrian crystal goblets to steal the show away from me," the devil leers. "Trade you a pair for that envelope," he barters, almost like he knows what is inside the envelope.

"TO HELL WITH YOU!" she blasphemes. With the acoustics being what they are, the execrating words echo off the walls of the Church of Pish and wake up the S/sisters, the lights and long dressing robes coming on in the cottages.

The jujubes weep ...

"What the hell is that down there?" the helicopter pilot asks the co-pilot.

"Looks like some kind of a maze."

"Why would anyone put a maze out here in the middle of nowhere?"

"Ah, you know these reclusive cult types. Probably trying to make some religious statement," the co-pilot says. "Brings the '60s back, man."

"How's than, man?"

"I went to Esalen in the fall of '62," the co-pilot says.

"What's Esalen?"

"Big Sur, man, home of the Esalen Institute, experimental workshop with no restrictions where social scientists did their thing on seekers of personal growth; Protestant theologians, advocates of LSD, Carmelite monks, psychotherapists, ESP specialists, Zen scholars, architects, Hindu mystics, wine tasters, perfume smellers, skin divers, mountain climbers, dancers, all walks of life, from kitchens, businesses, universities, law offices, and Haight-Asbury," the co-pilot says, the philosophy of here and now.

"That's heavy, man., Which one were you?" the pilot asks.

Cupping his headset, the co-pilot deepens his voice into the microphone. "Graduate student preparing a thesis on meditation."

Esalen: A healing place to amplify feelings, turn hostile suspicious individuals into trusting and aware people for more meaningful lives, and where a group of psychotics can be experimentally treated and allowed to go on voyages of discovery, their psychoses studied by social scientists here, refusing to subscribe to any dogma in religion, philosophy, or psychology. The Esalen Institute has common ties with what the pilots are seeing down below, that the individual return from the trip will be with a higher IQ and to cut through society's excessive verbalism to authentic feelings.

It looks like a spiritual carnival from the sky. Vi's equestrian labyrinth represents many tribes. Attached to six hundred wooden poles set into the ground forming a circle an acre in diameter are sticks drilled into the center of the poles; traditionally, the Kiowa sticks represent a pony to be supplied when visitors departed; from the Apache-Kiowa-Comanche Reservation are sticks symbolizing the peyote staff; the chokecherry sticks represent the traditional Hidatsa arrows; circa 1904 are the sticks representing the lance of the Cheyenne Dog Society; to tether valuable buffalo and horses outside their owner's tipis are the sticks that represent the Crow picket pin; imported from the land Down Under to the Tropic of Capricorn, taking a fix on the Southern Cross are the limbs of the mango trees made into walking sticks where the soul went walkabout on a *Dreamtime* journey; representing the hallmark of the Clovis culture are the sticks from where the Clovis spearheads are attached.

With a post-hole digger attached to the tractor, Vi makes easy work out of digging the holes. It takes fifteen weeks to dig the six hundred holes exactly the way she laid it down in ink. They take turns lifting each other into the tractor bucket to attach the sticks into the drilled-out centers of the poles, and then tie bright-colored streamers (no government red tape) on every stick some twenty feet high.

Words can't express what this all means to Vi. If the mustangs choose to participate, they will be making a spiritual contribution. Perhaps there is a personal need for Vi to build the labyrinth, but the value as a training aid is obvious.

"When do you plan to begin?" Sadie asks.

"As soon as I raise my spiritual IQ," Vi answers. "The mustangs will need me to be on their level. They will take me up step-by-step, not the other way around."

"Hon, you've got the highest spiritual IQ of anyone I've ever known. How do you mean that?" Sadie asks.

"These mustangs have lived in the most hostile of deserts. I need to connect to their environment to show that we have a spiritual bond. It's crucial that I memorize the path of the labyrinth knowing my way in and out without faltering the slightest. To do so will be a sign of mistrust in their eyes," Vi says.

Challenging and damn powerful, she has built the labyrinth to set a new pattern of relating to the natural world. Most have a concept of animals as lesser beings; Vi feels different. There are those who think animals can only learn through repetition and force. Vi's training methods will be with a level of understanding that the mustangs are individuals capable of a wide range of emotion and intelligence. She will give no verbal commands. She is prepared to find her common bond with them through meditation in walking the circle.

From The Convent To The Rawhide

Communication with animals through psychic ability — or the "sixth sense" — can come from speechless mutual recognition if the receptive minds translate words into thoughts in nonverbal communication.

Perhaps the story can be told best through the walking sticks attached to the poles in the labyrinth that represents Australia's contribution of *Dreamtime*.

The Outback story is based on a true account of a man's encounter with a tribe of wallabies, kin to the kangaroo. The wallabies have overrun a meadow the man has intended for his cattle. At night, the wallabies come out in great numbers, dining on the organic clover the man spent a lot of time growing.

Angry one night, the man takes his gun out to the meadow, prepared to shoot the wallabies and drive them off his land. He waits in his vehicle and when he hears a rustle, he turns on his headlights, seeing a large wallaby standing on its haunches. He puts the wallaby in the crosshairs, but can't pull the trigger. Seeming like an eternity, the man and wallaby stare at each other, until the man lowers his gun, allowing the wallaby to return into the darkness.

Something happens between the man and wallaby when they lock gazes — perhaps compassion and kindness. The next morning, the man calls out a message to the wallabies from his sixth sense of nonverbal communication. He feels their eyes on him, watching him from the big forest. He communicates to them he wants to make a deal with them — he won't shoot them if they will confine their eating to just the edges of his field, leaving the rest for his cattle.

Next, the man puts padlocks on his gates and tells the neighbors there is *NO HUNTING!* In the next few months, the field grows back nicely and the man is able to increase the size of his herd because of the availability of food. The clover is dense and although the wallabies have carved trails through the center, they don't eat what they have been asked not to.

Unfortunately, the story ends on a sour note. The man sells his land and moves away. The new owners take the padlock off the gate and allow the wallabies to be hunted.

Back for a visit, the man sees that the pasture is butchered along with the wallabies. The remaining wallabies come out in great numbers from the forest, angry, and wipe out the pasture.

This is proof that telepathic communication happens between humans and animals, and Vi intends on bridging the gap through the labyrinth. If the labyrinth can turn a wild politician into a different direction, then it can surely turn a wild mustang into a gentle communicator and companion.

The dedicated efforts of the S/sisters save the Pish Convent short-term, but its long-term operation is in great peril. With a keen sense of pooling resources, Sister Muriel and Sister Cavanaugh gather the S/sisters for a meeting to discuss Sister Pish's recent spell of Alzheimer's. She is resting comfortably in her private quarters, being in the twenty-four-hour care of a private nurse who has prescribed her the herb ginkgo biloba for her impaired memory, although Alzheimer's disease is not curable.

One of the sister missionaries is a lawyer on an eighteen-month sabbatical. To whom it applies, the sabbatical year affords one a leave of absence every seventh year for research, travel, and rest. She advises Sisters Muriel and Cavanaugh to request power of attorney. In agreement, they ask her to draw up the papers in the capacity of their attorney so they can submit their request to the court.

An operating agenda is discussed. Sisters Muriel and Cavanaugh feel they can carry on without abeyance. Violet feels it her duty to mention to them, "I have strong political ties and suggest that you ponder a land and conservation trust to protect future interest of the Pish property, disallowing new development; no new homes or convenience stores or radio towers. The drawback will be the land has to be donated first by Sister Pish, but the good that can come from it is the Sisters can still own the land and continue to ranch it. You can even sell it, but you and the future owners can't build on it, but you can remodel. In return, the donor can receive a variety of federal and state tax credits and breaks on inheritance and estate taxes." Violet says.

The theological debate over the environment for many years has centered on Genesis 1:28: *Be fruitful and multiply, and replenish the earth, and subdue it.*

Some interpret the word "subdue" as justification for development. Many others now view it as a mandate to protect the Earth in God's name.

"Religious scholars are saying to us politicians as we debate energy plans and protect the environment that we may want to consider how we will be judged by God, not just the voters," Violet shares. "I am in total agreement with this theology."

"We don't make a lot of money here, but we have so much," Sister Muriel says, "and we would like to keep it. We will take in advisement what you have offered. Thank you all for attending. We pray for you."

Mercedes thinks about the future of the Pish Convent all afternoon and when it gets to be about 10:30, just before lights-out, she buttons her long robe up to her neck and walks to Violet's cottage.

"Who is it?" Violet asks.

"Mercedes, but don't open the door, *please don't*, I just want to ask you something," she says, clutching a jujube.

"Okay," Violet answers, "but can I tell you what I'm doing right now?"

"Do tell."

"Stretching a canvas in my mind, dreaming of all the things about you I'd like to paint," Violet says. "Are you still there?"

Mercedes is closer than she has ever been to tearing off the mattress tag. "Yes. I want to ask you how long it will take for a land and conservation trust to go through if the Sisters decide on it."

"Anywhere from six months to a year. There's a lot of paperwork involved to create a conservation easement. It has to meet a set of strict protocols to qualify for conservation grant money," Violet says.

"Good night, Violet."

"Sweet dreams, Mercedes." Violet's cottage goes dark, then she reaches for her bells.

When Mercedes gets back to her cottage around the corner, she sits down and quickly writes a letter to her lawyer, requesting he purchase for her a charitable gift annuity stock issued anonymously to Sisters Muriel and Cavanaugh, that stock being Zions Bancorporation of Salt Lake City, parent company of Vectra Bank of Colorado.

The day comes when the pipe organ won't play. Mr. Linhart is also the rural mail carrier. Mercedes has a talk with him out by the mailbox today about why the pipe organ isn't being repaired. "No funds," he tells her. "The money set aside for preventive maintenance is helping pay for Sister Pish's care."

The 3,250-pipe organ has played its ethereal message on Sundays for forty years here on God's little green acres and Sister Pish told everyone the heavenly music is what makes the jujube trees climb the Stairway to Heaven, offering their fruit to those who earn their place in the Big Sky.

How can this be? Didn't Sister Pish get the check? Mercedes wonders. The devil knows what was inside that envelope. Remembering about when she had her attorney send it, she places its estimated arrival time at about the same time Sister Pish had her "Mad Scene" in "Lucifer." To remain anonymous, she has pre-arranged with her bank to have her lawyer send the cashier's check, the envelope having the bank's return address on it, and also the bank's letterhead on the letter describing the sizable check is to be used for pipe-organ repairs. Because telephones are not allowed and in this case the mail is too slow for what she needs to find out, (was the check mailed?) she goes inside the Church of Pish, where she always knew Sister Pish went to sort out the mail to deliver the sisters their letters.

Entering the Church of Pish is an open-door, everyday approach as opposed to "This is what you do on Sunday." It keeps no hours, only the faith.

Opening the double white doors and entering the Church of Pish is like going inside the Christian line of a Hallmark card; inspirational and spiritually versed. Those who go inside are really touched by this smaller, homegrown church.

It is a great church for simple purpose, belonging to all who visit. In the season of fruition, Eastertide is an especially nice time to come, the pipe organ raining down on the jujube blossoms, filling the air inside with the wonderful scent and sound of welcome.

And then there are the thousands of notes of color where gems of light play through the stained glass where Mercedes sees on the window ledge, a piping of silver light falling upon an envelope, the one where the need has never been greater.

There is no dishonesty in the way she chooses to handle it, only cleverness. She tucks the envelope in the middle of today's stack of mail that she has retrieved from the mailbox, volunteering for the daily duty. Maybe Sister Muriel won't notice the two-week-old postmark. Then she prays, kneeling before the altar, the prayer for growing older, written by an aging, anonymous Mother Superior.

"Lord, Thou knowest better than I know myself that I am growing older and will someday be old.

"Keep me from getting talkative and particularly from the fatal habit of thinking I must say something on every subject and on every occasion.

"Release me from craving to try to straighten out everybody's affairs.

"Keep my mind free from the recital of endless details and give me wings to get to the point.

"I ask for grace enough to listen to the tales of others pains. Help me to endure them with patience.

"But seal my lips on my own aches and pains — they are increasing and my love of rehearsing them is becoming sweeter as the years go by.

"Teach me the glorious lesson that occasionally it is possible that I may be mistaken.

"Keep me reasonably sweet; I do not want to be a saint — some of them are so hard to live with — but a sour old woman is one of the crowning works of the devil.

"Make me thoughtful, but not moody; helpful, but not bossy. With my vast store of wisdom, it seems a pity not to use it all. But Thou knowest, Lord, that I want a few friends at the end. Amen."

The humor in this prayer certainly will not be understood by a woman having thus far only lived for twenty-three years; she has not lived long enough to know these things told of middle-age, but to us forty-somethings, we can appreciate it, perhaps finding the better part of ourselves in those lines, thanking the wise woman who wrote it.

This brings us to another art — the art of giving gifts. The most important is the thoughtfulness the gift represents. Take a picnic, for instance; the one Mercedes is going to gift Sister Pish with. She takes her time to prepare the curried tuna sandwiches.

CURRIED TUNA SANDWICHES

1 6½-ounce can water-packed tuna, drained
½ cup salad dressing
½ cup finely chopped jujube (apple can be substituted)
1/3 cup raisins
¼ cup finely chopped celery
1 small green onion, finely chopped
2 teaspoons curry powder
16 slices cocktail pumpernickel bread
16 slices cocktail rye bread

She heats the raisins in 1/3 cup of water in a saucepan, adding the curry powder and boiling over medium heat for one minute. She lets the raisins cool for about thirty minutes, and then drains off the excess liquid before adding the salad dressing, tuna, jujube, celery, and onion to the raisins.

Charged with a sense of inner harmony, Mercedes spreads the curried tuna mixture on half of the pumpernickel and half on the rye slices and tops each with a bread slice of the same type. With care — because she does care — she wraps each one in a square of wax paper, molding and tucking the corners in, smoothing out the wrinkles for her friend, Sister Pish, and then refrigerates them until time, *time* being a word of special importance to the senior citizen: *Don't underestimate the time you may still have left.*

By the time the sandwiches cool, the jar of sun tea will be ready. She fills the jar with water and ties together three large decaffeinated tea bags inside, and then takes the time to walk it out to the grove of jujube trees, finding the most perfect sunny spot where she knows it can get four hours of God's strong sunshine in this spot before the sun moves and the shade sets in.

Being keenly aware of her creativity, it is here that God's little green acres show her how to make a picnic basket out of a small box by weaving some colorful paper twist from the hobby store, the many slumbering talents that are waiting within her to be unleashed. No television and no telephone free up just so much time, *absolutely necessary* to find one's set-point.

As she braids the handle with the paper twist, it must be said that at the same time, she is braiding *memories*. You will be surprised at how much warmth the basket will return in the future. To the person looking to deepen a friendship, they might just as well be on the lookout for a similar ripple effect of kindness that can spread (like the curry tuna mixture) beyond the original intention.

One of the best ways to deepen a friendship is to eat together. Many important deals happened when Jesus and his friends sat down at the table. There is something sacred in breaking bread with a friend.

Gluing the braided handle onto the basket bonded the Big S and the little s; the ages of the women are not important. This is a heartfelt picnic, so there better well be a fancy bow for celebration. Mercedes loops a wide strip of paper twist, fashioning a nice bow. The Mormon women make a lot of these two-color-checkerboard baskets. They fill the baskets with foodstuffs and give them to the new ones who arrive in their community. All of this comes from having an educated heart.

"I would like to take you on a picnic this afternoon in the jujube grove," Mercedes says. "Are you feeling up to it?"

"Can I carry this beautiful basket?" Sister Pish asks, her mind calm and operating normally.

"Yes, carry it to your heart, for that is where it came from — from my heart," Mercedes answers.

Mercedes spreads out a red-and-black checkered blanket and they sit down in the shade under the jujubes. "As clear and as refreshing as the Provo at Sundance running over the rocks," Sister Pish comments when Mercedes pours the sun tea over the ice cubes. The Provo River is one of the most beautiful rivers in the Western United States, good for year-round fishing, well-stocked with brown trout. "I always like to stop and fish the Provo on my way to Temple Square in Salt Lake," Sister Pish says.

"Who taught you how to fish, Sister Pish?" Mercedes asks.

"My beloved Daddy Pish. His grandparents, Papa and Granny Pish came here with the first party on the Mormon Trail with Brigham Young in 1847. Papa and Granny were just tiny babies coming with their folks in wagons," Sister Pish tells.

"Did they settle this convent land?" Mercedes asks.

"Yes, Sister Cade, they made babies of their own on these acres. Remember this: Bloom where you are planted. When the Lord called all of my family home, I planted this jujube orchard because I knew God would provide the time to let the trees make fruit for others to enjoy someday, and here we are," Sister Pish remembers, but that is the strange thing about Alzheimer's coming and going. The chances of developing Alzheimer's increases with age, and its frequency doubles every five years after age sixty-five.

What a picnic! A hot-air balloonist parks her wicker basket. She bends her knees slightly to avoid breaking them when she sets the balloon down. "I'm asking to tether my balloon. Unfavorable winds at five hundred feet forced me down," the woman explains.

"At ease in Zion," Sister Pish says. "Will it tear up the Lord's divots of grass?"

"Mercy, no! God has dropped out of the sky to assist me in his pasture," the woman replies, not knowing she has landed on convent property. "The Fisher pen was taken to the moon. It met NASA's and God's requirement, a gravity-free-flowing instrument for writing in outer space," the woman says, seemingly like she is offering this omnipotent ball-point pen for deposit that can write upside down in the sky, over grease, and underwater, *or* it is so almighty that she is going to use it as a stake to tether the balloon. Having learned over time to travel with this cavalier attitude, she is carefree and gay, the blithe spirit of a balloon pilot.

It isn't long before the chase crew arrives, communicating with her by radio. Balloons fly best very early in the morning when there is no wind and the temperature is cool. Wind means everything to a balloonist. Updrafts, downdrafts, and wind direction determines where the balloon will go. For that reason, the ground crew takes it down. Pushing the air out of the balloon and rolling the fabric into a bag is no easy feat.

The balloon basket and the picnic basket are emptied and packed up. At ease in Zion — until Sister Pish walks over to the chase truck loaded with the balloon basket and asks if she can carry the beautiful wicker basket. The jujubes weep...

The chores are done, for up to five days and the windmill is greased. They put the sign on the door, GONE DREAMTIME. The quarry is calling Vi, the archetypal place where she knows she can raise her spiritual IQ by flint-knapping spearheads and meditating on the Clovis culture.

Vi, with a leg fit comfortably on each side of her palomino filly, and Sadie astride her paint, each saddled their pony outfitted with martingales, big moon going down, and olives in their saddlebags. They set out this time in search of a higher spiritual IQ, known to be below the surface where the spirit marshal told them they could find their "missing hides," when they had converted from the Mormon religion to Australian *Dreamtime*.

What brings people to change religions is a variety of things: a spiritual crisis that can't be relieved by the person's original faith, or a major life change like a marriage, partnership, divorce, retirement, or relocating. Most converts are lured to their new faith by someone they have a close personal relationship with, which is the case with Vi and Sadie: They were one another's lure.

The Mormon faith is just too structured of an environment for Vi and Sadie to live with all throughout life. Vi wants to let the rebel wind comb her hair, fanning it out by playing a hand or two of poker in that same maverick air, and Sadie likes to masturbate and choose orgasm for herself without being told she "must not." She has thighs that can crack walnuts, strong and powerful and she is damn proud of what is lying between them. She is a damn good-looking woman and she has a woman who is just as damn good-looking as she is.

Sitting atop the ridgeline — where the charred remains of their bush telly is still visible from their last visit — Vi and Sadie look down into the quarry tailored by the habits of the Clovis people.

"Mark this one down with a notch of prehistoric IQ," Vi says, as she makes the conical fracture, flaking lengthwise channels in the chert they had found at Muleshoe. The chiseled stone sends her on a journey through the labyrinth prairie that lured the Clovis people across a thousand strange paths — mixed-grass, tallgrass, and shortgrass — tracking quarries of stone to make their prized spearheads needed to bring down the mammoth until they became extinct from overhunting and climatic changes that reduced the grasslands to desert scrub. On the Great Plains, water became scarcer and grass grew shorter and tougher where the advantage went to the lighter-footed grazers with thinner bellies and smaller thirsts.

The origin histories of the Plains tribes places their roots in North America, being what scholars contend that the earliest inhabitants of the Plains were descendants of the first Americans who crossed from the Old World to the New World during the Ice Age on a land bridge that briefly connected Siberia with Alaska. This temporary link was forged when the glaciers receded, opening a corridor south where the migrating bands made their way from Alaska and northern Canada onto the Great Plains where they found Ice Age animals such as the camel, giant bison, mammoth, and a native species of horse.

These animals eventually became extinct. The Plains then supplied a new quarry of the modern bison as well as small game such as rabbits, deer, fowl, and fish.

Then, a second extinction: The horse having ties with the Old World was lost from the American landscape, which had first evolved in the New World millions of years earlier and spread to Eurasia over the land bridge during the time of the glaciations. Its descendents repopulated the New World after the North American horse died out for the first time. After the second extinction, around 9000 BC, the horse was reintroduced to the Americas by European explorers. The great significance of the horse transformed the lives of the Plains Indians.

What this all has to do with the wild mustangs is this: Spanish conquistadors brought these first horses that resembled the wild mustangs from southern Spain. Over the generations, the Spanish Andalusian horses evolved into what we now call mustangs. These mustangs bore Spanish explorers across two continents and they brought to the Plains Indians the age of the horse culture. Texas cowboys rode them to extend the ranching operation to the plains of Alberta, Canada; Spanish horse, the Texas cow pony, and the mustang all one in those times.

The mustang will always symbolize the Western frontier. An estimated 50,000 wild horses still roam the U.S. public lands, a legacy from Spanish explorers.

In full gallop, nostrils flaring, the mustangs raced, their hooves hurling divots of shortgrass to escape the Nevada desert roundup by the BLM, created to keep their numbers in check, corralling as many as 10,000 a year for its wild horse adoption program.

"Listen — can you hear their rough breathing?" Vi asks, opening her mind's eye.

Their bedrolls are airing, swagged over the gnarly mesquite limbs and their horses are tethered in a nice patch of timothy grass for grazing. Sadie gathers up some loose mesquite branches that have fallen to the ground and breaks them into sticks to get the bush telly going for some campfire coffee. "Mark this one with a notch of outback IQ," Sadie says, making her conical fracture from *Dreamtime*. Giant of a storyteller that Sadie is, Vi asks her to tell her the Down Under rebellion story of Pigeon's War once again. She never gets tired of hearing it. It is a powerful story of the sacred mysteries of the *Dreamtime*, one that was passed on from generation to generation, to a gallery of Australian dream keepers in the outback — people who conform only to nonconformity. This is why Vi loves the outlaw Australian tale and the story that is partly responsible for their conversion from Mormonism to *Dreamtime*.

"Plenty of places for Pigeon to hide out here," Sadie says of the quarry landscape, mostly limestone outcroppings and slabs of volcanic obsidian several hundred feet down below in the quarry. She hears the spirit marshal's raspy voice, "*The rest of what is down there must be left to our imaginations.*"

For hunting and gathering peoples, there were places where supernatural ancestors went about their daily duties. Markings in the rock were identified as footprints or other human traces, taken as proof an ancestral being passed. The Australian ancestral beings Djanggawul and his two sisters were said to have sexual organs so long that they dragged along the ground when they walked during Dreaming, leaving their tracks on the rocks. In the Western Kimberly Mountains of Australia, the Aboriginals view an entire rock formation as the *wandjina*, the ancestors of the Araluli people who were believed to have turned to stone as they stood fishing for rock cod.

Similar rock-dwelling spirits belong to the Native American tribes. High rock outcrops are commonly seen as places close to heaven, like Spider Rock in Canyon de Chelly, Arizona.

The Judeo-Christian tradition recounts how the wife of Lot was turned into a pillar of salt during the family's flight from the destruction of Sodom, where slender salt rock outcrops were a notable feature of The Dead Sea in which the Biblical story was set.

In the New Mexico outback, the red-tailed hawks — a sort of prairie pigeon — wheel in the sky, until Sadie turns them into Aussie butcher-birds, their flute-like song drifting through Australia's coolibah trees. Sadie alerts all those interested that Pigeon's War is about to begin by blowing the didgeridoo she brought along, carrying the musical eucalyptus pipe in a rawhide gun scabbard. When they hear the low baritone drone, the Clovis spirits and Sky Heroes come alive in the cracks and cliff faces, and introduce themselves to one another. The Clovis trade their prized spearheads to the Sky Heroes for red ochre the Sky Heroes use to paint their millennia-old Aboriginal cave-wall paintings of the Rainbow Serpent, guardian of waterholes.

"We use this red ochre too," the Clovis spirits let it be known to the Sky Heroes that they, too, use the claylike material tinted by iron oxide for religious ceremonies where they believe in an afterlife, as evidenced by the burial sites near Wilsal, Montana where the bodies of two children were buried after being covered with the blood-red pigment. They associate it with the symbolic restoration of life. Also buried

From The Convent To The Rawhide

with the children were the Clovis spearheads believed that the children would have needed to journey to the next world.

It is time for Pigeon's War. "In the darkness of Tunnel Creek, the Aboriginal outlaw-hero Pigeon and his small band hide from those who hunt him for his hit-and-run attacks on the settlers who have stolen *Dreamtime* land from his people," Sadie starts.

Vi runs her thumb along the points she fractured into the spearhead to test its sharpness. Her dad used to take her arrowhead hunting before the antiquities laws came in, so she had really become interested in arrowheads when she was a young girl. She doesn't always get or *want* the same answers when she asks Sadie questions about Pigeon's War, but Sadie always tells it with the same outcome, embellishing it with different elements every time she tells it. "What is it you want to know about Pigeon?" Sadie asks Vi.

"I want to know about Pigeon's spiritual IQ," Vi replies.

"He eats intelligent mutton from a settler's station. He and his band are hiding from search parties. He drinks Shiraz wine from a kangaroo waterbag, tasting what will be his last liquid.

"'How smart are ya, mate?' Arrow asks, an Aborigine who has spent most of his life using a crowbar to dig for goannas, a lizard on his tucker menu.

"Kangaroo kebabs are Pigeon's favorite. He is eating them right now fresh off the barbie, spearing them with his knife in between bites of mutton. 'I reckon I be 'bout as smart as yellow dots on gray skin,' Pigeon replies, referring to the perentie, the largest lizard in Australia linked to *Dreamtime* where it is said the giant perentie ancestor sang the valley into existence on a walk through the northern Simpson. Yellow dots on gray skin make the lizard nearly invisible against the rocks. Pigeon's spiritual IQ comes from this *Dreamtime* lizard. On this day of Pigeon's War, it comes out to sun its half-grown body — longer than my leg," Sadie tells, tailoring this part of the tale just for Vi.

"Was Pigeon a complicated character?" Vi asks.

"Yes."

"Why?"

"Because he isn't a by-the-books man — and everything he does, he does with a passion for the environment and protecting the land."

Dreamtime converts are unique. They're having a bit of drama. Everyone you meet in a *Dreamtime* story will know one another, know *of* one another, or have something in common. *Dreamtime* converts pursue life as *they* see it. With the goal of self-determination, they learn from original stories where there is a whole religion built around *Dreamtime*, its emergence from the Sky Heroes, those supernatural ancestors from so long ago.

"Pigeon lights a hand-rolled cigarette with a piece of kindling in the fire, passing around the Shiraz made from Australia's most popular red grape, the wine known for its powerful plum, currant, and peppery flavor, Wolf Blass President's Select Shiraz is the favorite of the tribal council — a native mix of white, black, and brindle people who are hiding Pigeon, not out of obligation, but rather to confront the political state, defending the land, property, and hunting rights of the indigenous people."

To the Aboriginals, the land is more than a geological phenomenon, but a spiritual one. Human beings may be entrusted with guardianship of ancestral sites associated with the Dreaming, but the idea of "owning" the land means it is placing oneself above the Sky Heroes who created both land and people.

Sadie continues. "Whites come in and kill any game they want, but when an Aborigine spears a sheep or cow, he is branded an outlaw. Pigeon kills only when he has to. He is a tracker for the police. He gets tired of killing his own people.

He wants to be free, let the wind comb his hair, play a hand or two of canasta, so that's what he does. Pigeon has magic. He can disappear. Yellow dots on gray skin make him invisible like the perentie.

"Pigeon and Arrow are playing an Australian version of mumblety-peg called knifey just before dark. They see light coming from the bush. Constable Richardson — the elected crooked skink that he is — shoots Pigeon's uncle in the back. Pigeon's uncle is Arrow. A skink is a lizard from the rainforest that uses its bumpy, leathery tail like a fifth limb to grab onto things, like the way a corrupt politician grabs greed, going out on a limb for a bribe to line his lizard-hide wallet," Sadie says, giving the true story this notable addition, relying on what she knows to be the truth of why Vi quit politics.

"Bloody oath!" Vi cheers, Australian for that's the truth. "FBI, Ruby Ridge, Waco, Oklahoma City, Columbine!" Vi knows the stories, she's sat with Janet Reno to discuss them, but she always has to ask of this story at this point, "Is that what started Pigeon's War?" She knows it is hard to convince outsiders of *Dreamtime*, and she doesn't expect too many to find it.

"Pigeon shoots Constable Richardson, and then flees into the bush with this band of Aborigines where they start a small-scale rebellion called Pigeon's War. Pigeon loves to track the trackers who are tracking him, standing high above his trackers on a ridgeline, waving his spear and rifle in the air, taunting them. He holds out for three years, and then one day — without warning at the entrance to Tunnel Creek — he is shot dead in an ambush by fellow Aboriginal trackers. They say they took his head to Derby..."

What are the universal themes and linkage between modern-day politics and Pigeon's War? Perhaps we will find the answers when we raise our spiritual IQ's, when we "*be 'bout as smart as yellow dots on gray skin.*"

Amid the swirling dust and bawling cows, Vi and Sadie push their herd back in range when they notice on their way

Sage Sweetwater

back, the cows have drifted out a little further than they feel comfortable with. They both cover all assigned positions – the most prestigious job – the point rider – going to the most experienced in the outfit, then, a third of the way back from the pointer, the swing rider, and then, another third back, there's the flanker, and finally, the drag rider who brings up the rear. They alternate positions, the least desirable being the dragger who watches the south ends of northbound cattle. It's top hats and tails, whistles and "Haws!"

Some of the cows form a strong attachment to each other, so they walk with their companions until the end. Vi and Sadie have to rely on their mounts to get the job done. Their horses are so in tune they know when it is time to quit. Lightning is one reason to quit. With metal in their belt buckles and horse gear, Vi and Sadie are excellent targets.

Compatibility is crucial since these women eat and sleep together twelve months out of the year. They depend on each other for their lives. Courage and a Marlboro spirit can sometimes bring on a serious injury. An empty stirrup does these cowgirls no good, but nevertheless, born to the land, throwing her coil of feminist fuse and caution to the wind, letting the wind comb her hair, Vi takes off like some wild ass and independent mustang, hurling divots of buffalo grass, running back to the ranch at full horsepower, her spiritual IQ at its zenith. "Rawhide!"

The Mormon faith – more than most – emphasizes family roots. Members of the Church of Jesus Christ of Latter-day Saints have retraced the steps of the first settlers of the faith in Utah by trekking across the United States In covered wagons

From The Convent To The Rawhide

and on foot, pulling handcarts made by the Martin and Willie handcart companies pulled by the women having to go at it alone with the heavy handcarts when the young men were recruited into the U.S. Army to supply a battalion to fight in the Mexican War. The migration lasted from 1847 through 1869, when the Transcontinental Railroad was established.

Many lives were touched and testimonies strengthened from an early winter storm that struck the converts at Martin's Cove where the Martin and Willie handcart companies had sheltered the blast on October 19, 1856. Rescue parties reached them on November 1, but 145 members of the Martin Company and 67 members of the Willie Company perished from exposure and starvation before reaching Salt Lake. Giving a historical overview of the hardships endured by the original sojourners instead of a sermon, Sister Muriel says this experience gives meaning to the phrase, "Faith in every footstep."

Three of the sister missionaries will soon be leaving the Pish Convent to board one of the eight tall ships going by sea, commemorating the path taken by Mormon converts of Europe, Scandinavia, and the United Kingdom who came to America 150 years ago.

Some thousand modern-day Mormons are going on the fifty-nine-day voyage from Denmark to New York. They will be expected to work alongside the professional crew as trainees, doing things such as keeping watch during four-hour shifts in the middle of the night and polishing brass.

Mormons in the United States sent missionaries to Europe in the 1840s where some 85,000 Mormon converts crossed the Atlantic Ocean during the nineteenth century before finding their way to Utah.

The eight ships are set to sail from Denmark to Sweden to Norway, then on to Germany before arriving in England. Four of the ships are scheduled to cross the Atlantic via the Canary Islands and Bahamas, set to arrive in New York thirty-nine days later. One of the sisters will be sailing on along with a history professor on board to teach about the early immigration. For one of the sisters, the trip will have a personal meaning: A group of her ancestors emigrated from Croatia as early converts coming on a ship.

"I think it can be done, Sister," Sister Muriel says.

"How will it affect our community, Sister?" Sister Cavanaugh asks.

"We are an independent order, privatized by our own agenda. We will still give our tithe of 10 percent annually and live according to the Book of Mormon," Sister Muriel says.

"But what of the Catholic Sisters — where shall they tithe?" Sister Cavanaugh asks.

"They will give to their Catholic Church staying within the doctrines of their godly institution. The two religions must come together if we want to keep these grounds that are so beautified by the jujubes. We must remain fruitful, Sister."

The conversion will happen immediately. What does happen to aging nuns? Where do they go in old age? Who takes care of them? They don't have adult children to look after them. Most just stay in the system well beyond their working years working behind gift counters in convents that sell religious items to visitors to provide operating revenue.

Nursing home just doesn't fit. "We will convert the Pish Convent into The Orchard of Retreat. The sister missionaries along with a few skilled nursing assistants will care for the Sisters and we will make our jujube jam to sell in our gift store," Sister Muriel says.

"What gift store, Sister?" Sister Cavanaugh asks.

"The one we will pray for and ask God for a plan to remodel our retreat house into."

"What a wonderful idea, Sister."

The Roman Catholic Church declared that Mormon converts must be rebaptized, a setback for the Mormon

Church to designate itself as a Christian denomination. The Vatican's Congregation for the Doctrine of Faith says that baptism in the Church of Jesus Christ of the Latter-day Saints is not the baptism Christ instituted. The Vatican holds that the Mormon view of the nature of God is too different from Catholicism.

Despite its distinctive doctrines, the eleven-million-member Latter-day Saints Church is putting itself out there in America as a legitimate Christian church and missionaries are winning converts in foreign countries.

Sister Muriel has already checked into it and the Roman Catholic Sisters will be getting retirement monies from their Catholic institution to pay for their care. What difference does it make where the operating money comes from, or from what religion? It is all in God's will and salvation to help the Sisters who have Alzheimer's and to convert the ones who can no longer walk upright on their feet to a wheelchair.

Mercedes is leaving. Violet's new partner has already arrived. Julie Burnside is twenty-one and born to win. She cares about the world and its people. She is not isolated from the general problems of society, but is concerned, compassionate, and committed to improving the quality of life.

Emotions run high. It is a maze of feelings. Up until now, Violet hasn't thought about this day. Now that it is here, her heart plunges and falls right off the glacier peaks of Montana where she has butted heads with rock climbers who don't want to walk in from the road, so they make side trails with their vehicles, hundreds of them trying to find a crack to climb, scarring the land with their mountain bikes, ATVs, SUVs, and Jeeps.

"When I first came here, I wondered, what is it will I be doing here? I am leaving with a feel of the Big Open, my environmentalist friend, Violet Mace-Reese."

They stand for a moment, memorizing each other's lines around the eyes, mapping each other's face. "I will walk you

Sage Sweetwater

in the labyrinth of my mind every day for the rest of my time here, meditating on the intimate core of Mercedes Cade," Violet says, touching Mercedes' cheek with one finger, signing her name with the wet tears. "There...you're on the books."

"I'll write," Mercedes says, holding a three-peck pail of jujubes she is taking with her.

"No, please don't; it will make it harder," Violet says, her emotions raging.

It is easy to see how two women can become so captivated with each other. It happens when things are good, when you awaken to the brilliant sunshine and the smell of ripening fruit against a tranquil backdrop: *Zion*.

Mercedes gazes at it one last time. "I will call you in six months, Sister Cade," Violet promises. "Where are you headed?"

"To see some Mojave yucca and smell some cliff rose where there are no paved roads, where it's big and wild," Mercedes answers.

"Sounds like BLM's unpaved back country byways near Price, Utah," Violet says.

"Could be, sister."

The gearshift doesn't want to engage to the D. Finally, Mercedes drives off, watching Violet Mace-Reese in her rearview mirror drop to her knees with her hands extended out in front of her clasped together in prayer, whispering under her breath, *"I love you, Mercedes Cade."*

The market value of the Pish Convent — soon to be converted to The Orchard of Retreat — can't be bought with her millions in Colorado banks. Mercedes would just as soon turn around and go back to sign on for another term, but she has found her set-point, so it is time to move on. She drives just a little ways up around the red-rock outcroppings overlooking the Pish Convent, looking down at these timeless pieces of God's green acres. More than that, it is priceless. She can hear the organist testing the pipe organ as Mr. Linhart makes the necessary repairs. Life doesn't get any better than this — sitting atop the red rocks and stone spires listening to Mozart's C *Minor Mass*. Yes — Mercedes has made friends with her money, finding an answer to a question she had when she first arrived: How do you want how to help others with your money?

Lines of people form near Kanab, Utah. They don't have frayed tempers. They aren't standing in line for music tickets, but they are attending a "rock concert," where they are watching thirteen condors being released, their mellow stage on the Vermilion Cliffs in hopes they will meet up with the Grand Canyon condors in an attempt to breed in the wild. Mercedes takes a picture, thinking of Violet, the wind combing her wings. The condors come in a Forest Service aircraft where they are taken to Marble Canyon near Kanab.

"Claim your cliff, Violet, find your way back," she whispers, watching the condors adjust to the climate, location, and wind direction.

A peregrine spokesperson tells the onlookers that biologists re-released the Grand Canyon's resident condors earlier after treating them for severe lead poisoning where the scavenger birds ingested lead shot from an animal carcass. Violet won't like that.

Mercedes follows the drama. She watches the condors fight the cannibal buzzard for the salvage rights to a dead lesser buzzard lying in the desert in Page, Arizona, winging their way on to the splendid Grand Canyon.

En route to the Grand Canyon herself, there is another element at here; sixty-seven tons of structural steel, all of which had to be packed down to the river on muleback in 1928 to build the footbridge; "God's foothold," Sister Pish told her one day before her "Mad Scene" in "Lucifer," telling Mercedes "You have not completed your mission until you have walked on this footbridge." Located on the South Rim of the Canyon, the Kaibab Suspension Bridge, where earlier, there was no way for the Utah-based Saints of the Mormon Church to cross where they thought the river would otherwise eliminate difficult overland journeys and provide a faster route between their various settlements. Under orders from his church, "The Mormon Leatherstocking" explored the region, only finding crossings at the lower end of the Grand Canyon. He visited the Havasupai, "people of the blue-green water" living on the Canyon's floor, and learned their language as he did communicating with the Hopi, Paiutes, Shivwits, and other Indians, dealing with them by a code, summing it up by saying, "Never be angry with an Indian and always tell him the truth."

The Mormon Leatherstocking told the Indians the truth. When he left, intending to return in three weeks, he gave an Indian a leather bag with twenty-one beans. "Eat one every sunrise," The Mormon Leatherstocking said. "When the last one is gone, I will soon return." Indeed, three weeks later, he returned. Because he was so admired by the Indians, they would have told him secrets they kept about the Grand Canyon, and if there would have been any easy way across it, the Indians would have informed him, but there simply was no easy way across the Canyon. For that reason, the Mormons never succeeded in establishing a foothold south of the Colorado River, although the northwestern corner of Arizona, cut off by the Grand Canyon, remains Mormon country to this day, known as the "Mormon Dixie."

It will take a vision to escort Mercedes across the footbridge. She is uneasy about walking on the footbridge, just wide enough for a mule and strong enough to support a string of mounted tourists. Sunrise in the Grand Canyon is like a new beginning for the world. She prays to muster the courage to get in line and walk the footbridge.

Not everyone on the rim of the Canyon thinks of God. The poet Carl Sandburg did. He thought of divinity when he made the statement; *"There goes God with an army of banners."*

From The Convent To The Rawhide

Of the literary ones before us who wrote about the Canyon, Sandburg wrote the most and was the most excited, saying this is what he viewed; "battering rams, blind mules, mounted police, elephants grappling gorillas, cathedrals, arenas, somersaults of railroad train wrecks, exhausted eggheads, piles of skulls, mummies of kings and mobs, sobs of wind and water storms." Others do not see any or all of these things, but the first sight of the Grand Canyon is a shock, and the mind's pedal twitches for a while; "*God's foot upon the treadle of the loom,*" a handmade phrase of Herman Melville's, Mercedes praying to God, hoping there are strong fibers in the Lord's thread, referring to the eight 1½ -inch steel cables supporting the footbridge.

Mercedes sees a vision — a vision of such almighty strength; lion-colored, chiseled shapes of hard-body women, the cliff rose living in the fissures of their cleavage. Lost in admiration for the *lumberjills*, outsized ax-women crossing the footbridge on the way down to the canyon floor to the Colorado River where they train for "The Olympics of the Forest"; sawyers, pole-climbers and log-rollers, dramatization of modern-day logging. Mercedes disremembers her fear, instead concentrating on the burly women who smell wonderfully of the ponderosa fragrance of vanilla, the ponderosa bark containing the same chemical as the vanilla plant.

Packing their silver blades, backpacks, and canteens, these barrel-chested babes with forearms like tree trunks and tawny manes chant "Yo-Ho!" on cue, as a greeting and for fun on their way across the footbridge on their way to the Kaibab Trail, some of the lumberjills as far away as Australia and New Zealand, logging no longer dominated by rugged woodsmen from the north country.

The lumberjills are physically fit, athletes who can make it down in one day from the Kaibab Trail. It descends 4,800 feet in 6.3 miles and crosses the Colorado River near Phantom Ranch, where a lot of hikers break the trip, although four days is a much more reasonable length of time for side trips, photography, and contemplation.

The Paula Bunyans have permits to cut an area of ponderosa pines for spinning logs on the water with their feet, their lumberjill training for the Lumberjack World Championship. The Park Service is sponsoring "salvage logging" to thin out the small trees that are reducing the survivability of the large ones, the small trees a potential high-octane fuel for fire. "Yo-Ho!" Mercedes hears the lumberjill echoes from the canyon walls down below as she walks back across "God's foothold." She disremembers her fear, instead concentrating on brilliant midday colors of the Canyon walls. It is October, "the month of burning leaves," the leaves in nameless shapes in red, gold, pink, orange, rust, mauve, and a good many other colors, those same brilliant colors of the plaid-flanneled ax-women, lumberjill haberdashery. If you're looking to get to the other side, where the cliff rose lives in the fissures of their cleavage, *Yo-Ho, lumberjills!*

A house is not a home if it does not have food and fire for the mind as well as the body. The home is where we seek a haven from a world moving at the speed of light. This concept lends the proponent of less-is-more philosophy in housing where small homes foster closer family ties. A small home places parents and their children closer together where spaces have to be learned to be shared and where one learns respect for the needs of others. In larger homes, children exist in their own world with their own television, telephone, radio, and computer where there is a limited need to share or for family interaction. This makes families grow further apart and less communicative. Think of it in this way: Drop the multi-bath option that means more sinks and toilets to clean when you can be relaxing in family-friendly spaces that are cozy and welcoming, where even the teakettle sings from happiness: *that* is home. God bless it.

Indicative of the good life in nineteenth century America, the picket fence is making a comeback. To have, or to have not a fence; it either keeps something in or out, but the *white picket fence* has been much more. For generations of Americans, it came with the American Dream of home and hearth, and represented a way of life in simpler times.

The tumbleweeds clog the falling-down barbed wire fences. As a symbol of desolation, tumbleweeds thrive on wounded land. Despite the tumbleweed's place in Western lore, it is also called Russian thistle and is native to Asia, not the American West. Its arrival came a few decades before the arrival of groundwater pumping.

Abandoned farmland is not much to look at – rusted pumps, discharge pipes, and a windmill in a sad state of disrepair. Farmers should plant perennial grasses before departing farmland, but few do. How do you tell a bankrupt farmer that they have to take care of this one last agricultural task? Mercedes wrote this letter to Violet with no intention of sending it, honoring Violet's request:

> Tumbleweeds have invaded this abandoned cropland; could be setting the stage for a new Dust Bowl. Please come and help me with this land I have purchased, which is extremely susceptible to wind and water erosion.

The real value of the Pish Convent is in its meadows of grazing deer, antelope, grouse, and a coniferous scatter of pinion pine and numerous other scrubs of bushes and trees for the habitat of wild birds. In alignment with Sisters Muriel and Cavanaugh's wishes, Violet is prepared to file a conservation easement deed. She is surveying the three hundred acres, explaining to Julie Burnside the how and why of a land and conservation trust.

"This easement will protect river banks from eroding, save it from subdivision development, protect the historic structures, and protect migration routes and habitats for wildlife," Violet tells Julie. "I am very glad to see this land go into a possible conservation easement. These acres lie within a very important migration corridor for the native wildlife."

Being both intelligent and keenly aware of an alliance between Utah soil and Mormon settlers is what makes Julie Burnside say, "Seems like these acres lie within a very important historical migration corridor for Mormon settlers." Julie is from Moab, once a Mormon farming and ranching town. She is a writer for the local newspaper, *The Canyon County Zephyr*. She took a leave of newsworthy absence to come here.

"Yes, you're right, Julie — namely the Mormon settlers of Pish. They took pride in this land for what it holds of the beauty of God and spiritual redemption," Violet comments.

Julie is a sweet girl. She puts her arm around Violet and says, "Some would say this will make a nice golf course or a row of condos — it's what has happened to Moab."

"Won't happen *here*," Violet says with certainty. "We're about aligning the Sisters of golden age with The Orchard of Retreat." It sounds pretty eternal, where in this community, the gerontologists are doing the Nun Study of social and psychological factors in that there is something about the act of caring for others that seems to enhance one's vital spirit to successful aging and that life-giving generosity is *alive* and well.

Differences in vitality can be traced partly to genes, random patterns of inheritance that accounts for much of human diversity. Aging is more than biology, life history, genes, and environment. It is hugely a matter of sociology — of how one shares the experience of old age with others, which contributes to the quality of life and longevity. It seems that the secret to aging well is to find a balance between trying to stay young and accepting the temporary nature of life.

Quite busy in her golden age, one of the graying Sisters is in the retreat house kitchen making jujube jam. She takes great pleasure in making jellies, jams, and in canning fruits and vegetables, derived from her career as a home economics schoolteacher before she retired and came to the Pish Convent some twenty years ago to live out her old age with an orientation toward the future, gratitude, forgiveness, optimism, empathy, and the ability to reach out to others.

Nobody will argue that religion is a comfort to the troubled, a friend to the sick, and a constraint on the wicked. A woman should always strive for three things: evenness of temper, steadiness of mind, and a flow of humor, which is the Holy fire that keeps our purpose warm and our intelligence blooming. "Women give themselves to God when the devil wants nothing more to do with them," Sister Pish has always said, demonstrating a nun's humor before Alzheimer's robbed her of her mind.

Sister Muriel — with her soft soul, sharp eyes, and full head of mature hair — retrieves the day's mail and goes inside the Church of Pish to sort it, keeping with tradition. As a member of the aging-nun community, she recognizes the practicality of having a guardian angel. It is the quintessence of Eden. Every day, she prays in earnest for a gift store where the Sisters can exhibit their jujube jam in a cubbyhole cabinet for all to see and a glass apothecary cabinet to dispense their medicinal jujube cough syrup and a restored farmhouse buffet with maple shelves to cool their homemade pies and some hand-forged nails to hang their picture frames proudly displaying their artwork — some religious, some inspirational, and some humorous.

Today, her prayers are answered. Most beautiful things in life come by twos and threes, by dozens and hundreds, but inside this special one envelope, it comes in thousands: the Zions Bancorporation annuity, the funds for remodeling the retreat house into a gift store. No tear affects Sister Muriel's eye more than the joyous tear of this donation.

For now, the tumbleweeds can stay. They provide top-notch winter cover for pheasants. In winter, pheasants utilize four basic habitats; feeding, roosting, shelter, and loafing areas. Russian thistle or tumbleweeds are good cover when they pile up in dense mats against wire fences or other obstacles.

Come springtime, I am going to pull out the fence posts and roll up the "Devil's rope" to break down the boundaries to merge so that some other force may take place, Mercedes wrote to Violet. She is sealing the letters in envelopes to give to Violet to read when she can see her. *I am going to purchase a herd of Brahman-cross cows and I am going to breed them for their perfect hides, free of scars and brands, valued highly by leather furniture consumers, paying for the perfection and coddled lifestyle of the cow. Please come and help me watch over my herd. I want to be your cowgirl.*

With a wealth of original details, punctuating the farmhouse's interior, keeping with the well-balanced theme of pine wood and wide-plank pine floors, pine paneling, a drop-leaf pine table and ladder-back chairs, and an original deacon's bench with storage under the bench seat where Mercedes is storing the letters she has written to Violet.

Being mesmerized by the Southwestern sky and New Mexico's bold skyscapes is what inspired Mercedes to move from Colorado where she has a desire to preserve the ever-shrinking piece of ashcan life that remains.

She is cross-stitching on a muslin curtain that works well against the pine backdrop to dress the windows. Windows are a reflection of her childhood, where in one part of town, a fringe of families lived below the poverty level. The able-bodied ones — given to sloth and idleness — taped the broken window panes with gray tape and had wild boys who threw dead 'coons on the porches of black families. Remembering this all throughout her life, she always keeps her windows clean and dressed and is especially nice to Negroes *and* raccoons to make up for the decadence and prejudices.

Now that she is in between religions, for the time being, she is going to worship the cowgirl and the old tradition of living on the land. She is going to try life in the saddle, try to understand how it works, then paint it on burlap with a sheaf of wheat — the burlap not the kind in a cloth store but the kind you find on a feed sack.

There is a new bonanza of psychology, a feminist pronouncement that says a woman needs to reach a healthy level of self-esteem before putting on a cowgirl hat. One thing more: courage, strength, stamina, and spirit weaves a common twine in the lives of modern-day cowgirls who exemplify the spirit of the Old West.

Taking into consideration the cowgirl's stride, she needs to decide how intensely she wants to live the cowgirl lifestyle, by choosing it through the type of boot she wants, height of the heel, stitching colors, toe shape, and pull straps. Just how much of a custom fit of a cowgirl lifestyle does she want? Does she want her boot heels layered up with wooden pegs and side stitching done by hand and the welting put in like it was a hundred years ago, with a curved awl, one stitch at a time built by a modern-day bootmaker keeping true to the old-world ways who makes the boots by hand? How about a pair of vintage cowgirl boots like the '50s originals, cut, molded, and stitched by hand like the pair sold in Sundance Catalog?

Already the feminist idea of the modern-day cowgirl is snubbed in Cheyenne, Wyoming. A forty-foot-tall neon cowgirl with a coil of rope over her shoulder towered above a proposed Old-West-style visitor's center luring tourists downtown was abandoned because the menfolk want no part of her. Perhaps she is just a little too real for the male culture. Those sleeveless western midriffs on a hanger on a thrift store rack are disappearing as fast as the employees can tag them and ring them up.

How much testosterone polishes the 485-foot-long set of horns towering fifteen stories above a highway in Fort Worth, Texas to commemorate Texas livestock drives, marking a cattle route that once fed into the Chisholm Trail. You can bet the horns are staying, and they should, right along with the neon cowgirl in Cheyenne. They go together. Women went up those great cattle trails working the big cattle drives of the Old West, working as trail hands while their children rode in the chuck wagons, and some even had their own herds.

Before Mercedes leaves this plane of life, she wants to try the life of a cowgirl. It is a trip she wants to make. This very thing incites other women to want to go, especially the younger girls who look up to women who are on top, riding in a saddle with a good fit on feminism. She is a keen-looker full of reserve and at trail's end, she wants it said that she downed a plate of prairie oysters she harvested from the lead steer in her herd, but that is down the trail a ways. For now, the trail menu consists of the "three B's" — bacon, biscuits, and beans; the bacon known as "overland trout," the biscuits, "hot rocks," and beans, "Pecos strawberries." Canned milk is known as "canned cow." Western artist Charles Russell said that the only milk they ever had was Eagle Brand, which "sure musta come from that bird. It's a cinch it never flowed from any cow."

Sapphic Sex and the Single Mare: This demands absolute patience and skill. Ride her hard the first few nights to tire her into submission. Let her graze before bedding down. It is imperative not to crowd or spook her, otherwise it could spark a stampede by stepping on her tail during the night. The cowgirl — who follows the trail, her mount, the cowgirl poetry that she writes and recites, what she does and *how* she does it — is left to other cowgirls to give them their proper place in modern-day society.

Come gather 'round me girls,
And I'll tell you a tale;

I left a lady in tears
And I said that
In a Western novel
Where sex and religion
Ride together;

Racing to control
Her spooked heart
Was only part of her troubles;

I quit her in
The monotony
Of the chase
And instead, bought
A handful of hearts,
Rough-hewn pewter,
Tokens of affection from
Sundance,
To tuck under my pillow.
Whoopee-ti-yi-yo!

Andy Sue rides the asphalt hard. Her Harley is geared for this mission ride. Fourteen months ago, she had her sprocket changed for highway miles. She follows the paper trail now and then when she gets a lead. She's put new rubber on twice, so you can imagine her resolve.

The buffed pretty girl composes her aura. In headband, silver-studded gauntlets, and full leathers, she looks like a medieval warrioress ready to lift the sky for a moment so she can find what she is looking for underneath. She will be terse, clearly expressed, then return to her home where she owns a high-end gym salon and oxygen parlor exclusively for women — and ever after — live happily as walking advertisement for her stylish commercial establishment.

She is obsessed with shaving her legs, cunt, and underarms daily with mineral oil from a special basin, a baptismal font from the Amazon that she worships. She grows her hair on her head long, looking like a medieval warrioress fighting cholesterol wars and raiding fast-food restaurant deep-fry vats.

Out of novelty and mainstream science, inhaling scented oxygen from a "facial cascade," a Darth Vader-like hood over her face keeps her alert and social; again, Andy Sue is a walking advertisement promoting that purer air is beneficial. The air we breathe contains only 21 percent oxygen. Depending on the method of delivery an oxygen parlor uses — a plastic tubing apparatus or a hood — the equipment can provide up to 99 percent oxygen.

"A sturdy woman who looks as though she may have been created from the Lord's stone is asking for you. She is dressed in black, seated upon a two-wheeled machine. Her dark hair is tangled from the wind. When I said I'd come for you, she was putting on a lovely shade of lipstick seemingly like she was making herself presentable to you. Do you know the identity of this woman?" Sister Muriel asks Violet.

"Indeed I do, Sister," Violet replies. "The woman who accelerated my retreat."

"Go speak with her, Sister Reese, tell her what it is we do here. Offer her a guest cottage for the night if the wishes to stay," Sister Muriel says.

"Thank you, Sister." Of course, she would come. The time is right. The paperwork is done. The conservation deed is filed. Violet thinks for a moment; *She will be low-fat butter on my toast, articulate, try to influence me by using a psychological recipe — an ounce of lust, a pint of exhibitionism, and a gallon of narcissism.*

"You're a long way from home, Andy Sue," Violet says.

"I've spent fourteen months hopscotching the pavement looking for where you dropped your rock. The chalk trail led me here. Hell, Violet, you're my wife!"

"We substitute 'South Heaven' for the H word here, Andy Sue. How did you find me?"

"The paper trail to the taxi cab that brought you here. A convent! It might as well be China, Violet!"

"Come to my cottage, Andy Sue."

"Here — I brought your favorite shade of lipstick."

Never caught up in the politics of Andy Sue, all the legislation in the world cannot abolish kissing her — but the Pish Convent can.

"It's been black moons and pale skies since you left. Everybody's working on something, Violet, abs, pecs, biceps, what are you working on, huh?"

"Disappointments and corruption of life," Violet answers, painting her lips. "Andy Sue, you have to free yourself sometimes to find the basis upon which you can build an *important* life work. You have to ring the sleigh bells, call the reindeer by name," Violet says, handing Andy Sue one of her weighty handbells. Andy Sue hasn't a clue as to what Violet has said.

"I remember waking up in the dark in a sweat, feeling for you, but you weren't there. One year and two months, I played with myself. I think great stuff comes out of being alone. Buffed and up at daylight hovering over my baptismal font of mineral oil, shaving, and oiling."

"But do you have a life outside of this narcissism, Andy Sue?"

"It is very hard to live up to my vainglory reputation. Gallantry is one of my traits. Come back with me. Hop on the back of my bike and we'll ride home together. I brought your leathers."

Finishing a commitment was never a problem for Violet. Just shy of four months left on her mission, she feels like she has more than served her time:

> The dove has returned to her olive branch. She has not breached her commitment, but rather has found her answers four months early. Rest assured she will get back to Montana safely before the snow begins to fall. A convent is as good as its Sisters. You are all wonderful. The conservation

deed has been filed. It was a pleasure to survey all of God's creatures that roam this property. Good luck with The Orchard of Retreat. You should receive the grant money by early spring. God Bless you all and Sister Pish.

She left the letter on the table in her cottage. After dark, they ride off, the buffed medieval warrioress on her iron horse thinking she is rescuing her queen, living up to her vainglory reputation. But it just isn't true.

After a week of wearing a facial cascade showering her kisser with eucalyptus mist oxygen, Violet soon has enough of scented oxygen-enriched air and listening to the high end of lame, buff conversation; *amour-propre*, also know as affluent narcissism, drifting just a partition away with the pungent smell of cooking spray, oils, and lotions mixed in a dizzying combination, bodies and egos in the making.

Violet hasn't seen Andy Sue since they got back. And there is no sex between them. Most of these women have cold, lonely bedrooms. They are obsessed with warm, anointed muscle — not sex — and when they do have sex, they have it with men from other gyms and other women — one-night nothings providing an ego boost for powerful people — threesomes, foursomes, and moresomes, keeping it in their own group of strengthy socialites, power-lifting politicians, and big-name professional wrestling Amazon women.

Being blunt, Violet is nothing more than "arm candy" to Andy Sue, a post-sexual image enhancer and ego booster. One evening two years ago, Violet walked into the trendy gym for a workout to relieve stress over politics. Andy Sue introduced herself and the evening turned into stone. Violet was craving hard sex with another woman and Andy Sue is a sexual stone, just a fucking rock of a woman; an ass and thighs beveled out of basalt from a primitive pick made from Montana antlers, arms resembling bluestone pillars from a Druid temple at Stonehenge, breasts built like Silbury Hill in three stages enlarged with chalk blocks in sloped steps to form the mounds in-filled with chalk rubble, and protruding from her tight spandex top, megalith nipples chiseled out of granite, hard, Violet thinking she must be careful not to chip her tooth on one.

All of this buffed perfection and Violet would rather have the delicate curve of Mercedes Cade, so she calls her. "What!" The telephone in Colorado has been disconnected. Home four months early, craving quality conversation with Mercedes Cade and Violet can't get in touch with her. "Let me work on this — I can fix it," she tells herself. "Damn!" I want her." She looks, but nowhere do morning glories twine around the door. "DAMN!"

She has to get out of the gym, go somewhere and think. She needs a lighter world. She puts a high premium on privacy. If there was a labyrinth in sight, she would walk it. If there was a planetarium nearby, she would observe the stars projected on the dome ceiling to be closer to God's heaven, anywhere but here! She especially likes the mountains, sunsets, flowers, trees, animals, and the howl of wolves answering the coyotes, the unspoiled and the original. She appreciates the natural world. She doesn't seek out taverns, night clubs, parties, smoke-filled rooms, or *muscle conventions.*

She let her apartment go, sold her furniture, and put her car and personal belongings in storage before she went to the convent. Andy Sue wants her to move in, but that's a big no! Each of us desires a place we can call home, and we also have the feeling of being an outsider. It doesn't take long for her to find her lighter world.

ANTLER, PAW, HOOF, FIN, and WING
Studio loft for rent ONLY FOR ONE MONTH
Above taxidermy

It takes her just a few hours to set up a temporary studio in the loft. She grabs some things to paint with. The loft even has a corner fireplace she is definitely going to enjoy. She's had a chill inside her every since her and Andy Sue got back. Riding a motorcycle in the month of December through Idaho is unkind to the veins. They ran into snow just across the border out of Utah into Idaho, so they rented an *Easy-Ryder* with-a-heater moving van and put the Harley in the back. Violet bought herself a cord of hardwood mix for Christmas. She'll use whatever firewood it takes for the month and leave the rest for the other tenant who is coming at the end of January — the loft is only available short-term.

Violet has always wanted to paint wildlife and right downstairs there are plenty of wild animals, ones with the finest glass eyes she can stare at and study for hours without them making a move.

In front of the fireplace on the floor is a bearskin rug and there are zebra-skin shades on the lamps. The first night, Christmas Eve, she sleeps on the bearskin rug. The fire is going warming her thoroughly from the mean chill she hasn't been able to shake. It is strange how certain environments can warm the spirit instantly, mostly those that come from nature. Violet feels a world of difference here compared to the gym.

Christmas morning, taxidermist and landlord, Tyler Roger brings her a roasted goose in a green casserole dish covered with tin foil with a red ribbon. "Merry Christmas from the wife and me," he says. When Violet reaches out and accepts the dish, freeing up Tyler's hands, he reaches in his pocket and gives her a goose call. "Called it in with this," he says. "It's made out of walnut." He shows her how to use the three reeds, adjusting the call to air flow and style. She likes the raspy Arkansas-style reed the best. "It's yours," Tyler says, "For the goose on the loose."

"Thanks, Tyler — and tell your wife thanks — I appreciate the goose to go with my cranberries."

"What do you paint, Violet?" he asks, noticing she has her easels set up.

"Are you going to be here for a minute?" she asks. "If you don't mind, I'd like to take a few Polaroids of the stuffed animals downstairs so I can draw an outline, then when you're here after the holidays, I'd like to come down and paint them," she says.

"Here — take the spare key and go on down after I leave. I think I can trust you," he says. "I'll be with *kin* — not family — for a few days," he says, making it perfectly clear, "this *here* is my family — antler, paw, hoof, fin, and wing."

"I don't know — I was a politician," she teases, "think you can still trust me?" Tyler doesn't recognize her even after she signed her name to the lease, and she'd just as soon he doesn't. He looks genuinely like a young Robert Redford in *Jeremiah Johnson*, a young thirty, case-hardened, bearded mountain man who wears fur, fringe, and buckskin, blending in just so ruggedly handsome with his Montana lodge-style taxidermy.

"Depends on what you did after that," he grins, entertained by watching Violet run a can opener around a can of cranberries, cutting the circle out of time. The annual holiday clock is always set by the opening of a can of cranberries.

"I was a Mormon missionary at the Pish Convent in St. George, Utah."

"Sure, Violet," Tyler says, not believing her. "Practice your goose call and I'll look in on you in a few days. I'll pull the blinds so Montana Santa won't think I'm open for business and come for the stuffed animals when you hit the lights. Watch out for the Griz!"

Yellowstone moose, Canada's Hudson Bay polar bear, Dall ram taken from Alaska's Wrangell Mountains, Absaroka Beartooth Wilderness grizzly with Alaskan salmon in its mouth, and Montana elk bugled in and bagged by Jonesy Rich, a vagabond gold dredger and hunter famed for enormous harvests that made it into the *Boone and Crockett* record book.

Violet looks it all over — and — puddle duck! All of this wonderful selection of *big* trophy game animals and Violet doesn't seem particularly overjoyed. It is the cinnamon teal that catches her eye, a beautiful waterfowl. Teal are fond of puddles. The old term "puddle duck" is perfect for teal.

Following the intuition of her inner artist, she checks the mobility of the teal. She wants to take it up to the loft and paint it immediately. It looks like it is willing to participate. She can't remember ever a Christmas where her inner artist took over. It wants something from her: That is, to work toward a balance with a minimal amount of inner opposition through this stuffed teal, by painting it with her non-dominant hand, which is her left. Painting the teal with her non-dominant hand will let her overcome her insecurity about her artistic ability, because actually what she is looking at here is a creative experience that will convince her to turn wildlife art into a profitable hobby and still stay in the politics of endangered species and wildlife protection through portraying nature on canvas. She can still sign her name, only this time with a different standpoint, *Vi Montana*, one-woman show, building a reputation for fine wildlife art. So she starts on Christmas Day by the fire with a plate of gratis goose to go with her cranberries and a cup of hot apple cider with what will later become the plum of waterfowl art by winning an award and national recognition as well.

The two women for whom this novel is sagatized partnered up not so long ago. They each have a healthy Marlboro spirit. In feminist terms, we like to think of the term "Marlboro spirit" as meaning when a woman of a certain age discovers her "wild girl." There's no set stage, but at an age around forty, she finds herself doing things like climbing twenty feet up a tower with her grease gun in her holster to quiet the long-drawn squeak of a slow-running windmill. It is a time in a woman's life where she is drawn to the rawhide, which has been de-haired and cured, but not tanned. When rawhide is soaked in warm water, it becomes pliable and dries in whatever shape it's given, just like a woman. That quality makes for Western.

Riveted and outfitted with Western names that fit as tight as their Wrangler blue jeans, Sadie Cade and Vi Montana go off in the spring one day to the sale barn, after Vi read Sadie's letters that are stored in the deacon's bench. "*I want to be your cowgirl*" is quickly adhered to, they becoming each other's wrangler escort, cowgirls in the making.

At the sale barn, they each register and get their bidding card. Way before the sale starts, they look over the livestock. Sadie looks hard for unflawed hides. There are some nice young cows, but they are branded, taking away from the idea Sadie has in mind, thinking these cows will never do because their hides are flawed. For someone wanting to just raise beef, they are excellent stock, but not as cover for furniture. Sadie can go ahead and bid on them, then breed them and wait for

From The Convent To The Rawhide

next spring's calves, but it will take too long to grow them. She does not want to take this route. She wants to be building furniture covered in full grain by fall time. She'll have to pass on the cows for today, the brand inspector not particularly who she wants to see.

You can buy just about anything at an auction — from sleigh bells to the horses that give them their jingle.

"Six hundred bid, now seven, will ya give me seven? Seven hundred bid, now eight, will ya give me eight?"

Vi holds up her bid card. She wants to saddle that palomino and she wants to have those sleigh bells to ring and call the reindeer by name.

"Damn, cowgirl," she tells Sadie, "that rodeo clown bidding against me — we'll just put him out of the arena." So Sadie starts waving her card wildly trying to knock the clown out. She does.

"Eight hundred bid, now nine, will ya give me nine – going once, going twice, SOLD!"

The auctioneer's chant isn't all that difficult to understand once you develop an ear for it. It's a series of numbers connected by filler words to give buyers a little time to think between bids. You just have to listen for the numbers, the amount that has already been bid and the next dollar amount the auctioneer is calling for.

Before handing over a saddlebag of cash, you want to be sure you are buying a horse to meet your needs. When choosing a horse, you need not spend top dollar, but you want a horse that won't be plagued by lameness. You should be looking for a horse with a long shoulder in which the shoulder bone slopes more toward the rear of the body. A horse that has a short, strong back with a well-muscled loin area will be able to work hard over long periods of time. The loin muscle is critical, as it is the only skeletal attachment between the front and rear of the horse. A mount with a weak loin area is less able to push off its rear legs and move with as much power as a horse with a short, strong loin.

The horse needs a neck that sits reasonably high on the shoulder where the bottom of the neck should meet the chest no lower than half the depth of the horse's body. If a horse's neck attaches lower than it should, it adds more weight to the horse's front, decreasing its agility

One more important point in choosing a horse to ride is leg structure. If a horse has a crooked leg, the bone column doesn't align from top to bottom and the horse can't bear its weight equally across the joint surfaces, this can make the horse prone to lameness. You want a horse that has legs naturally set under the four corners of the body, just like how Colorado, Arizona, Utah, and New Mexico set under the sky at the Four Corners. Rear legs that set out behind the horse produce a less coordinated stride. Front legs that are set too far back shift the horse's body mass to the front, which again, decreases its agility — a candidate for lameness.

The last thing to consider is choosing a horse is to find one with a good disposition and quiet attitude, something that starts at training. Again, eyes are a good indicator of horse temperament.

One day a little later in the spring, still no cows or horse for Sadie; they go off to Ten Thousand Village, a Mennonite project where baskets, carvings, linens, and nativity sets are crafted by Mennonite artisans in thirty developing countries. Separate from the booths, there is an auction to raise funds for global help, sponsored by Mennonite and Brethren in Christ congregations in Colorado and New Mexico, but is not a proselytizing effort. On the auction block is a refurbished old Ford farm tractor that doesn't have an obnoxious backing-up beeper (thank God), the one they need, and in less than an hour, the one that is theirs. The owner is going to deliver it to them the next day. Excited, but still no cows or mount for Sadie, she smiles and says to Vi. "Make no little plans; they have no magic to stir a cowgirl's blood."

No sooner than she says it, Vi looks out the truck window not believing what she is seeing, the kind of *amazing* thing she can put to an acre of canvas and hang it above the fireplace mantel in the farmhouse. By now, Sadie has noticed the maize-maze. No plain statement will do. "Corn fuck me! Think like a field!" Vi says, flinging the truck door open when Sadie pulls over.

Cornfield mazes are a growing trend, where farmers are drafting custom designs on a grid, then tilling paths in the field when the corn is tender and short, tending the crop as usual. This is a seven-acre corn maze.

They get lost in the sex in the big middle of it. Thinking like a field — as Vi told her — Sadie kneels, undoing Vi's jeans and plants a row of kisses, watching Vi's clitoris sprout around her tender growth of pubic stalk. Finding her way around the pink labyrinth, she walks Vi's labia in circles with her tongue, laying the groundwork for Vi's orgasm.

"I'll build it if you'll *come*," Sadie says, tilling a deep path with her tongue, thinking of creamed corn. It is a tasteful comment. Sadie makes love to Vi in a field of dreams where a hundred unbranded Brahman-cross cows are grazing in a neighboring holding pasture, gathered and offered for sale; thank God, the hides Sadie has prayed for. It must be quite a relief.

In the following days, Sadie and Vi take down all the barbed-wire fences that are loosely connected on the thousand-some acres, the letting go of the self in the presence of something vast and timeless. To live on this land is to be in line with the unbridled Clovis spirits of the Southwest. Looking to a horizon without any fences crisscrossing the land or scarring the cows is in line with simpler life and in search of the perfect hide.

Sadie has found her paint filly attached to some peeled poles tied together, what appears to be a cast-off of an Indian travois. The paint horse is a prop being used by the Mescalero Apache Tribe for the Painted Maiden Ceremony — a puberty ritual for six young girls entering womanhood. Sadie makes the deal around a bonfire at dusk after everything is cleansed in a ceremony with dancers.

With spiritual significance, Sadie gives the name Painted Maiden to her new horse who will be partnered up with Mavericka Bonanza, Vi's palomino. It is time to cowgirl up on those excitingly different Ozark Rancher's Basketweave saddles with rough-out fenders, skirt, jockey and a three-inch duckbill horn and quilted seat. Forget the traditional look.

Now it is time to get rid of the Dust Bowl, giving some thought to the tillers, sheaths, and nodes, the parts of the grass plant.

How grassland forms depends on the environmental factors like temperature, soil type, rainfall, and humidity. The grasses are divided into three types based on their height: tallgrass forms on moist soil, growing between four to nine feet; shortgrass lives low in dry soil, growing half an inch to only a foot-and-a-half; mixed grass is a mixture of tallgrass and shortgrass varieties.

Sadie and Vi plant orchard, smooth brome, foxtail barley, and timothy, grazing grasses to provide forage for the cows and horses.

They hitch a modified potato planter to the tractor with Vi sitting on the planter regulating the flow of seeds coming down the chute. If you're wondering how these two women get so much accomplished in a season, the answer lies in this: They are patient, and put their land smarts to work at an old-time pace.

At the same time Princeton University hires its first female president, the Orchard of Retreat receives its first Catholic nun in retirement.

Thirty-two years after Princeton University first admitted women students, it hired a senior molecular biology professor as its first female president as the school's nineteenth president since it was founded in 1746. In 255 years, the Ivy League college has had only eighteen presidents. Congratulations, Shirley M. Caldwell Tilghman!

Sister Claire Mulhaney, age seventy-five, has stirred quite a controversy for her massage ministry she practiced in Minnesota. Rooted in her Catholic beliefs, she teaches massage techniques, stressing a mix of biology and spiritual healing. She's been giving massages for thirty years where the naysayers say massages are not nun-like, but more on the order of the "red-light district."

Sister Pish made friends with Sister Claire and they often go to church together to listen to the organist, who is Mrs. Linhart. Mr. Linhart put in some new pipes that produce sounds of strings, flutes, and trumpets to full-throttle basses upgrading the tone quality of the pipe organ.

Some days there are more wrinkles in Sister Pish's memory than others. Sister Claire helps her to smooth out the wrinkles and stay calm. Combined with dishtowel therapy and Ginkgo Biloba, things don't get too out of hand.

Because of their ages, these two Sisters grew up with dishtowels where the dishwasher was a woman, not a machine. They each share their thoughts on when they pick a fresh dishtowel out of a drawer and how excited or dismal they become with what the pattern or picture on the towel reveals. Stripes and checkers are boring, making the chore of drying dishes unexciting, while ones with fruits and vegetables or cats or pigs or flowers make the chore fun. So Sister Pish and Sister Claire decide to make exciting dishtowels with a graphic spirit and hang them on a clothesline in the gift shop. Who wouldn't want to buy a dishtowel made by a nun?

Modern-day meteorology technology can't replace the nineteenth century weather vane. The history of weather vanes forecasts every civilization's interest in knowing which way the wind blows, and were once particularly important to farmers, fishers, and travelers.

The weather vane is a symbol of folk art and they show just so much more style than hanging up a wind sock. Prancing horses and farm animals predominated the golden age weather vanes advertised in a flier published by Cushing & White in 1872, which are prized by collectors, especially the ones that were made by hand before factories began mass-producing them.

You need not spend thousands to buy an old vane. Look for them at flea markets, auctions, and antique stores. You might pay less for one with considerable wear and tear, but they still might be usable in the garden or roof if they aren't too fragile or too valuable to be placed outdoors.

The Amish weather vanes are crafted from rural images, intrigued by the simple ways of the Amish and the vanes have no N-S-E-W directionals for this reason.

Sadie and Vi are installing the vanes they bought from the Mennonites. Not many modern-day houses are built with that crowning touch of a weather vane. The farmhouse and barn have the perfect roof line for the utilitarian art and whimsical cow, horse, and pheasant.

"Looks like Jediah and Zea," Vi says, pointing from the panoramic view from atop the barn. It is. They are riding up the driveway in the coach.

Sadie and Vi put their memory in rewind of how the coach looked before and notices it was complete in its restoration now. It's what Moses wanted. This is a day of sorrow. In the back of the coach is a casket. Moses is inside. "We're driving on to Ten Thousand Village. We'd be graced if you two kind ladies would ride with us to the service," Jediah speaks softly without emotion. "Papa Moses passed on."

"Can we have a few minutes to clean up?" Sadie asks.

"Jediah tells it right. We'll wait for as long as you need. Moses asked that you accompany us to his final resting place," Zea says. She is a gentle woman so precious in the kind, thoughtful, blue eyes of Jediah. The kind of woman he will look for those same genteel qualities when he is ready to take a wife.

Whether it is traveling to distant villages, knocking on doors, presenting the tenets of the Mormon faith or riding in a coach pulled by a team of horses carrying a casket on the way to Ten Thousand Village for a Mennonite service and burial, the spiritual journey is routed in search of the perfect hide.

Out of respect for this one time — and because it is the thing to do — Sadie and Vi put on their navy dresses that fall below mid-calf and their white blouses that cover their cleavage, the same set they wore in their missionary days.

On the ride to Ten Thousand Village, Sadie and Vi learn why Jediah has grown up so quickly: his Papa Moses was diagnosed with prostate cancer two years ago. Papa Moses tired out easily, which is why he took a nap while Sadie and Vi recovered the coach seat with Zea lying with him should he pass then. When Papa Moses said, "take away the power lines and the blacktopped country roads, my good Lord," he was asking God to see him to heaven where there are no power lines or blacktopped country roads, not letting on he was in such great pain. Moses got his wish to see the coach completely restored before his passing.

Ten Thousand Village closes down the craft booths and the Mennonites sing Amazing Grace. There are some kind words spoken about Moses. The bearded men dressed in Pilgrim haberdashery carry Moses' casket to the gravesite for burial in their private cemetery. Jediah discusses with the men his thoughts on the gravestone, which they make soon after one of theirs passed. As a witness to a compassionate God, there is a simple meal given to Jediah and Zea and their two guests.

Jediah is strong enough to carry on no matter what. The two draft horses are showing early signs of lameness. He will keep his eyes focused on the pastures and prairies, looking for a pair of work horses, preferably young — so he can train them to pull the coach his way — with an even temperament and proud to pull the Lord's wheel, Jediah's customized horse-drawn religion. Rest in peace, Moses — it was good to know you.

Horses gestate for almost a year. Three of the mustangs have foaled. Two of the mares had foals that each have an identical hay hook pattern on their foreheads, or is it the letter J?

Sadie and Vi assume the stallion is the sire. They soon find out he is when a woman — one Tracy J. from the BLM — drops by after seeing their name on the wild-horse permit.

"That stallion is kind of a legend in the wild herd," the woman who is a wild horse and burro specialist says. "Up until you brought him in, he was looking for new mares to gather. These are the mares. He lost his place in the herd. I'm sure you've noticed he's deaf or close to it. I spotted him with these new mares and the next time, he was by himself, and then he turned up again at a haystack we use to capture the wilds."

"He's got symptoms of frostbite on his ears, probably being a winter colt," Vi says. "But he's got a healthy dick; thought I was going to have to put it in the dirt on the way in."

The woman laughs at the hard feminist comment. "That's what we thought, frostbite caught the tips of his ears about five years ago," she says, confirming his age.

Wild horses need to be managed to assure a healthy habitat for all the other animals sharing the lands where wilds roam. The wild horse roundup ensures there will be adequate food, shelter, and water for all the wildlife. Meeting the goal to keep the desert ecosystem in balance keep range managers busy, as wild herds tend to increase by 20 percent each year.

The stallion that has impaired hearing or older horses that are not a good candidate for adoption are released back onto the range. Younger horses that meet the criteria are trained for dressage such as Marine Corp mounts, Westernnaires, or to use for 4-H, Girl Scouts, and Boy Scouts.

Age selection has a tendency to leave old horses with a lower reproductive rate and breeding time and no one wants them or impaired horses. Tracy J. doesn't agree with the current BLM policy where younger horses are captured and the older and impaired ones are turned back onto the range. "You just don't manage a healthy herd of any animal by removing all the young and returning only the aged," Tracy J. says. "I'm just happy that you've got the stallion. I've captured him twice, but had to turn him lose, him not being an adopter."

"We think he's got a personality fit for a maze," Vi says. She and Sadie tell Tracy J. what their method of training will be. "I walked a labyrinth at the Capitol and in doing so, it sent me in a new direction, so we're thinking if it turned a wild politician into what you're looking at today, it can surely turn a wild mustang into a gentle communicator and companion."

They take Tracy J. to see the equestrian labyrinth. Vi takes her place up front, then Tracy J. and Sadie follow at the back in single file. Vi walks them through the labyrinth that she has memorized so well, her spiritual IQ within a few days of being ready for the challenge. Vi stops at the pole with the stick drilled into the center that represents the hallmark of the Clovis culture. She climbs to the top of the pole. "What's she doing?" Tracy J. whispers to Sadie.

"Let's watch and see," Sadie whispers back. "That's the Clovis stick."

When Vi reaches the top, she locks her legs around the pole, and then reaches into her jean pocket, pulling out the spearhead she notched at the quarry from their last *Dreamtime* at Pigeon's War. She figures now she is 'bout as smart as yellow dots on gray skin and with that said, she ties the spearhead on the yellow streamer.

"I have an answer for you," Sadie whispers to Tracy J. "She's raising her spiritual IQ."

Tracy J. has another reason for visiting other than meeting the adopters. "After seeing what I've seen, I think you two cowgirls have what I'm looking for. I could use you ladies for a couple of days," Tracy J. says. "I have a question, so I better just ask it. Would you be interested in coming with us on a mustang roundup?"

Dust fogging and divots of shortgrass being uprooted from unshod hooves, pheasant locomotion, mare snot, stallion sperm, dry throat, keg of dynamite, lit match, coil of feminist fuse, *Sagebrush Rebellion*, frazzled and dirty as a street cleaner's broom?

"HELL YES!" Vi and Sadie say simultaneously, cracking their lips in a conspiratorial grin. Putting their memory in rewind, they've been on *that* ride. They aren't going because they *have* to or even *want* to. They are going for other women's daughters because they have no daughters of their own. "Make no little plans, they have no magic to stir a cowgirl's blood," Sadie says, making big bedtime plans with Vi. Ranch women go to bed early for a reason, and rise early for that same reason. Sadie and Vi were smitten with each other long before they could be together, so they don't let any pasture grow between their thighs. Hell, they keep it worn down to the nap!

At dawn, they load Painted Maiden and Mavericka Bonanza, that mare duly named for a wealth of rebel feminist. Sadie and Vi meet the BLM caravan of stock trailers and about thirty minutes later, turn on a washboard road splattered with a warm sign of mustang. Doing that horse-speak thing, the horses in all those stock trailers let out their arrival whinnies. Now is a good time to either confirm you have a sturdy mount that can go the distance and ask that same thing of yourself, or back out and read about it in *Western Horseman*. Yes, there will be writers and photographers and reporters and helicopters and a white 1966 Cadillac hearse and don't forget the Judas horse.

Tough as a pinewood knot combined with their Marlboro spirit, Sadie and Vi are good to go. So inclined, they snug their chin straps laced through the eyelet holes in the crown of their cowgirl hats. Saddled up and spurred, the rough thrill of mustang running is about to run out of fuse.

BANG! GO! RAWHIDE! The match has been lit.

"Here they come!" hollers one of the wranglers, throwing his hand up. An old Bell 47 helicopter with a bubble canopy swoops low over the wild mustangs covering them with dust from the wash of the propeller, the chopper pilot having a little fun. The pilot flew a copter just like this one in Vietnam. He's found the wilds a little earlier than usual this morning. Now it is all up to the runners to bring them in.

The trap is set up five miles from here where long walls of hanging burlap netting hangs between gaping rimrock set up ahead of time to funnel the wild bunch into a hundred-foot corral of portable steel fence panels.

This is where the Judas horse comes in. The Judas is so named because he will betray the wild herd, leading them to a hiding place right near the funnel and wall of burlap netting. You can't look at the Judas as a traitor. He is a friend to the mustangs, helping them onto better pastures where they will be adopted by those who will give them a simpler life, taking them out of the harshness of the desert and prairie where they will have adequate shelter and can eat grain and good-quality hay instead of settling for forbs and shrubs.

The Judas was a wild himself at one time. That's why he can do his job so well. He knows the terrain and all the tricks of survival and he uses his survival instincts in these roundups. The Judas is let out of the stock trailer under the turquoise sky. The photographers click pictures quickly with their more-frames-per-second motor drives attached before they lose sight of him, and the writers groom old-day words, sepia-toned and copper-colored words that won't need edited when they make it that far because they are at the top of the list of intelligent mustang clan symbols, the dust polished off mustang-speak with red bandannas, Western words fit for a Western happening; "squaw-hold," "15-hands," "dude string," "*Sagebrush Rebellion*" — where the pavement ends and the West begins!

Keeping up with the pace, Sadie and Vi follow the other wranglers who are riding hard, their horses leaving big hoof prints six inches into the ground and throwing divots of sod. About four miles out, it is getting exciting. There must be about thirty mustangs, thinking they're going to give the outfit total destruction, sheering steel posts, ropes, netting, and flesh — horse and human interlopers.

"Our kind eats pitchforks and barbed wire," they communicate with their devil-may-care attitude. Just look at them — their ears all pinned back, tails whipping, and nostrils flaring, trying to look mean. Right about now, one of the wrangler's saddles breaks in half. It's no time to have a weak saddle tree. He dangles from the piece that won't let go, looking like a piece of ham on a string.

"I'm OK — my daddy ate dynamite and washed it down with mustang!" the wrangler says, "Well, hell, bring 'em on in!" he cackles when his world looks level again. "I surrender!"

The mustangs start to split up. If you force them too much, that's what happens.

"Back off!" Tracy J. yells. "If you want to get them all, you have to let the Judas work it out."

Meanwhile, the wranglers who are waiting at the trap are doing a last-minute inspection of the burlap netting. They whip off their cowboy hats replacing them with baseball caps, the caps harder for the mustangs to see when the wranglers are on foot in the sagebrush.

The helicopter appears again on the last leg of the run. He doesn't like to run them over five miles per hour because at this stage, they are pretty much exhausted. The Judas heads them straight to the trap. One of the wilds isn't fooled and crashes through the burlap netting and escapes at full pace back into the desert. Two wranglers head on after him, they're right on his hocks shaking out their lariats.

"Missed him!" the wrangler says, disappointed and exhausted. "We'll get him on the next one."

Funneled straight from the burlap netting, the wranglers shuffle the caught ones into the makeshift corral. "You still with us, cowgirls?" Tracy J. asks Sadie and Vi. They are the only three women and one of them is running the show.

"You put all this sweat and energy into it, and one day, someone thinks they're going to come along and sweep it all away, but they can't — it's embedded in your soul," Vi says.

"I couldn't have said it better myself, cowgirl. Our whole life is tied to the land. We grow what we want," Sadie agrees.

"It occasionally gets caught up in red tape, but there's no other life for me. Each one of these runs holds a different drama. Most don't even know this exists. It's a powerful agent for those who commit, and there's a responsibility that goes with it," Tracy J. says, sharing her point of view. Sadie and Vi admire Tracy J. for her straight talk. "Work's not done yet, girls."

Sadie and Vi dismount, the foreman's son collecting their reins to water and tether the horses. He hauls a five-hundred-gallon water tank in his truck and another truck hauls two stock tanks to accommodate the thirst of the twenty-some tame and twenty-nine wilds.

The helicopter lands and the pilot comes on over to help with the branding, vaccinating, and worming done right away. They use a hot shot, running the mustangs one at a time through the squeeze shoot, and while the mustangs are standing, the wranglers quickly brand them with a freeze mark using liquid nitrogen, giving them a shot and a liquid wormer. In the morning, they will be loaded into a forty-foot trailer pulled by a diesel and taken to the BLM's Wild Horse Corrals for adoption. Six of the older horses are going to a trainer to get the horses started right for a "dude string." An outfitter with Rawhide Defenders has an application on file. The adopter must be at least eighteen years of age, a resident of the United States, and have no prior convictions for inhumane treatment. Adequate facilities and finances also must be available to provide for the number of wild horses or burros adopted.

"Day's done!" Tracy J. hollers. "Anybody need anything?"

"COLD BEER!" is the group chant; Tracy J. knows what they'll say. She's been with this wild bunch on too many of these overnight runs not to know what their request will be at the end of the trail, but she has to ask it anyway because she always likes hearing it, knowing a hard day's work is done, and she never fails to give her appreciation. "Thanks to all of you for a job well done."

The roundup cook has charred buffalo on the fire. It tastes right with a night of storytelling around the campfire where they are all on the same page. You must be able to hold it all in your mind. Nothing too serious — rope burns, smashed fingers, two wranglers with a bruised ego for the one that got away, and one saddle bit the dust. The art of the chase — once a runner, always a runner — guess we'll go again.

Vi is not campaigning the hearing-impaired stallion for a high score award or purple Rosetta, one of those big colorful silk ribbons. She isn't a "point chaser," where a good horse is pounded into the ground to earn points to win an award at the end of the show. The stallion has green status. He's grown into himself and into his bones and now it is time for him to grow into his tame spirit. It just is.

She's managed to loop a rope halter around all seven in the last few months. Most likely, it has to do with the way she and Sadie speak in low tones and whispers around the mustangs. The equine voice lies in their ears. Silent, but ever-responsive, the horse's "voice" delivers its thoughts and moods. This is why it is going to be a challenge with the stallion's cropped ears. They don't have the height to "read" them. One thing's for sure, he kicks at anything in front of him, and that's where Vi has to be to guide him through the labyrinth. There is a great deal of trust when inside a circle.

Before attaching a rawhide rope to him, Vi sits down to meditate on her spiritual intelligence at its highest IQ. She doesn't want to out-think the stallion, she wants to think with him and she wants him to think with her because she has some things of quintessence to communicate. She has a lot of respect for the mind of the horse and the buffalo, both being what she thinks superior to the mind of the human. Let the telepathic journey begin.

From The Convent To The Rawhide

His harem of mares isn't quite sure of this. In their eyes, he is being led astray by the new mare in the gray midriff with yellow snap buttons to match her spiritual IQ. Vi reads their ears, communicating to them that they will get their chance to go to the carnival.

She attaches the lead rope to his halter for her to hang on to and attaches another one to a buffalo skull that he is just going to have to drag along with him for the symbol of the Plains spirit. She mind-whispers about maverick independence, communicating to him they both have the same need for wide-open spaces. She looks him straight in his eyes, and with that communicated, she leads him slowly to the opening of the labyrinth which faces east toward the sun, intended this way.

When they reach the opening, she lets the lead rope dangle a little freer, communicating to him they are honoring the sticks, each one risen in respect for what each individual one represents. She stamps her foot lightly, communicating to him, "be guided by them."

Because she needs both of her hands free to make the Indian sign for "a long time ago," she lets go of the rope to show him trust. She makes the sign slowly with her hands, beginning at her waist, angled lightly to the left with both index fingers extended, her right hand drawn back to the right, looking him straight in his eyes. She is telling him a story from speechless communication.

She takes the lead rope back into her hand, looking up to the sky at all the colorful streamers, "telling" him about color and movement, and then she continues on through the circle; the six hundred poles self-hypnotizing, the totality of the labyrinth, an intoxicator of the highest spiritual IQ, a real mind bender.

Being able to "talk it" while walking it lets the both of them feel each other out. When Vi does the sign for buffalo where she places her hands at both sides of her head with her index fingers lightly hooked like the horns of the buffalo, the stallion moves forward, dragging the buffalo skull, then stops for her to pick up the lead rope. She begins to communicate this to him; a long time ago, the buffalo — just about then, and they are nowhere close to completing the walk where the manger is placed with timothy and grain, he is agitated by the bark of a prairie dog. Vi leads him back to the barn because he has done so well up until this point and she doesn't want to sour his first time out. Besides, she has to go cry in private. He acknowledges he is "listening" by moving the buffalo skull, showing her he knows what she is communicating — a long time ago, the buffalo — she sees him strain to move his deformed ears, just like someone with a speech impediment who stutters, trying so hard to get the words to come out.

The next day, after his first time out, while it is still fresh in his mind, Vi invites the stallion to escort her to the carnival. The mares are better with it today. Before attaching only the one lead rope, Vi scratches the wide space between his eyes. He stands fifteen hands (about sixty inches) and weighs around a thousand pounds. Every chance she can, she makes eye contact with him. "Are you up to it today, Outlaw?" she communicates. He's got a world of try, Vi is convinced, watching him strain again to move those cropped ears. Whoa! Back up! This horse isn't deaf. Vi puts her memory in rewind. Yesterday, didn't we say "he was agitated by the bark of a prairie dog?" How did it agitate him if he didn't hear the shrill bark? The little Gunnison prairie dog wasn't even in sight. Opinions vary widely, but watch him this time out. This includes every would-be animal psychologist who thinks a horse is an unthinking four-legged beast.

Again they stand at the entrance facing east. Vi stamps her foot lightly communicating to him about what the sticks represent and how the tribes used them in different spiritual ways. "Obey them," she mind-whispers.

From The Convent To The Rawhide

Now chronologically, the stallion's age is five, but historically, he dates way back, even before the mid-1600s where his ancestors were carved and chiseled into rock art. Vi takes him on a journey back in time. She "tells" him about Newspaper Rock, a twenty-foot-wide boulder in Utah, which is a miscellany of handprints, bighorn sheep, buffalo, footprints, weapons, and horse and rider etched in the mid-1600s when the Spanish explorers brought the horse to the Americas. "See there — your legacy on stone," she communicates as they walk the acre circle.

What do we know about rock art? We know that animals are featured prominently in the earliest known forms of human art. Some pictorials are etched or incised, while others are painted with natural earth dyes such as ocher. We know that they are not just simply decorative, but possess some more specialized, spiritual purpose. They are also thought to be a lasting means of record-keeping and to increase game supply and promote fertility through supernatural forces, and for marking cyclical events such as summer solstice. And we do know that the rock art created in the Southwest has been preserved by the arid climate.

The stop at the stick representing the Crow picket pin where the Indians used the sticks to tether valuable horses and buffalo authenticates a yesteryear television and magazine advertisement; put your memory in rewind. Visualize the tear of Iron Eyes Cody, the famous Indian who showed us cultural emotion. Do you remember seeing him crying that iron tear?

Communicating her emotion to the stallion at this stop is the spiritual quintessence of petroglyphs. Vi is outraged at the vandals that wiped out the priceless Blue Buffalo rock art in Utah recently and this is an opportunity for her to vent her feelings.

Vandals scratched a panel known as the Blue Buffalo, destroying the priceless petroglyph created over two hundred years ago in Utah's southeast desert. The panel can't be replaced because it was chafed with a rough surface, possibly scratched into the sandstone with another rock.

The Blue Buffalo is unique because of a couple of things. First, blue paint was less common than red or brown in those days, and secondly, the buffalo did not typically roam this particular area of the petroglyph, which means the artist was most likely from the Ute tribe and had the ability to travel.

For whatever reason, the Native Americans created rock art, religious or artistic; we should respect that. Imagine that it could have taken as little as fifteen minutes to destroy something so spiritual left by an earlier culture over two hundred years ago that had been so well preserved because of the climate.

Now Smokey Robinson said in a song that "there's nothing sadder than the tears of a clown." Oh yes there is! The tears of a wild mustang "listening" about Blue Buffalo vandalism, walking a maze to find his gentle spirit. When Vi looks into his eyes, he is crying and she will swear it on a stack of spearheads and join Pigeon's War, recruiting modern-day archaeologists with BLM who say there is just too much rock art to fence off all the sites. Can you see it – the archaeologists armed with their rock picks, standing high above on the rocks, shaking their primitive war picks at the vandals, wearing their hard hats prepared for The Millennium Rock War?

It is a wind-borne dust devil that spooks the stallion the second time out. It is behind him and horses can't see behind them, so he *hears* it, the swirling whoosh of wind-speak that makes him jumpy.

They walk a little farther today, but still not reaching the destination where the manger of grain and timothy is. Vi's emotions show on her face. She hasn't spoken with Sadie in two days. It is just too conflicting with speechless communication and Vi thinks it best to remain silent while she is taming the stallion, but she needs to talk out loud to

From The Convent To The Rawhide

Sadie — share her emotion about the vandalized Blue Buffalo. It is a big deal to her and if she was still a politician, she would sign a bill to impose stricter penalties for those individuals or groups who violate nature, including the graffiti artists. And she wants to tell these graffiti artists a thing or two; if you want to leave your message on the rocks, do it in a way that will help other generations learn positive knowledge from society, not just a bunch of gang symbols that stand for negative nothing! Be proud of your cultural art and share it with the rest of us on cultural days, in museums, fairs, and art galleries.

Fencing the sites isn't the answer. Those rocks don't belong fenced in any more than Vi or Sadie do. Not fencing in animals and sites should teach the people to search for human perfection, free of scars. In search of the perfect hides is what it's all about!

After the chores are done and it is nearing evening, Sadie goes to the bedroom and fills the oil lamp and trims the wick. She knows just how to comfort Vi tonight. While Vi is meditating in the old claw-foot bathtub on tomorrow's walk in the labyrinth with the stallion, Sadie places a gift on the bed she bought for Vi some time ago. She ordered it from Sundance, and has waited for the perfect time to present it to her.

"What's this, cowgirl?" Vi asks standing relaxed in her robe, combing her hair. Damn, she is pretty.

"Open it up and find out. I bought it for you quite awhile back. We had a conversation about a spiritual place where you'd been and I remembered that I'd seen this in Sundance Catalog. I think it will calm your emotions," Sadie answers. "And warm the room, too," she adds.

What it is inside that box all rolled up is an intelligent rug made by hand by the Tibetan refugees in Nepal. They used the neutral tones of the Southwestern desert to accent the figures of ancient petroglyphs sketched by a Utah textile artist in a joint venture with the refugees. And guess what? There is a sketch of a buffalo clipped into the design of thick, plush pile. "Sadie, this is the most beautiful piece of wool I've ever seen! I will cherish this rug always."

"Put it on your side of the bed," Sadie smiles.

"Okay." Vi puts the rug pad down, a protective pad to prevent excessive wear and the transfer of color, then lays the rug down on top of it. She lies down on the rug, wallowing on it like a buffalo cow in heat. Sadie lights the oil lamp and turns out the light and they make love right down there on the rug, the soft petroglyphs tickling their butts, humping buffalo-style, them using their heads as shovels *going down to get the grass*, wild and free-roaming — The Great American Buffalo Hump.

"Good morning. Applesauce and brown sugar can sure sweeten things up," Vi says, feeding Sadie pieces of her applesauce muffin.

"Give me one of your brown sugar kisses to wash it down," Sadie says. Vi cuts it short. There is someone knocking at the door.

"Well howdy, little lady, you look like you've got a range spirit. Buffalo Fence Company, ma'am — livestock fence — safe, low-cost, recycled old tires, veterinarian approved. Total package includes tire cutter, punch press, wire benders, crimpers, rubber winder, and instructions. Buffalo Fence machines are portable, clean, and easy to operate and carry a six-month warranty — and, we offer financing on approved credit — how about it, ma'am?"

A lot of good that does him. This is a good example of what we don't need. Now things would be a little different might he be selling a three-heart, blued-steel spur, silver inlaid, 2¼" shank with 2" fourteen-point rowels.

"Good luck with the stallion this morning, hon," Sadie says, knowing this is the last she'll get to talk with Vi for a while, respecting speechless communication. Now is a good time for Sadie to read some of those Louis L'Amour dimestore paperback novels she has stacked up. He tramped the Four Corners to put accurate details of the land in his stories. She'll start out with *Mustang Man*, and then put it down about half way and saddle into *Jubal Sackett*, the one that was on the *New York Times* bestseller list for nineteen weeks. His Western novels hit the marketplace at three a year. Not bad for a good-looking, rugged Frenchman whose dad changed his own name to LaMoore to make it less French.

Living on their thoughts, it is a predictable process, Vi and the stallion keeping this taming method growing and in short order — a little bit each day, nothing forced and if for nothing else, an entry in *The Diary of a Mustang Tamer* by Vi Montana.

"See there — the dove has visited — look at the sign she has left in your hoof print," Vi communicates by mind-whispering, showing the stallion the dove tracks that stamp the dirt with miniature peace symbols. "'Go in peace,' dove says," Violet communicates, making the peace sign with her two fingers. "Coyote and raccoon, too." The stallion keeps on playing follow the leader, that is, until the shadow of a passing cloud spooks him his third time out. It isn't so much the shadow that spooks him as what is flying in it — a noisy bubble with a long tail and a whirligig spinning on the top of it — like that thing that chased him into a wall of burlap netting. Putting his memory in rewind, he can feel his hide peeling right off his bones and his mane and tail being sucked up by that noisy magnet of steel.

"You might as well call yourself Pegasus and grow wings, because that's the only way you'll get out of here," Vi mind-whispers to the stallion when he breaks the lead. She just backs up and leans against the Kiowa pole with her arms crossed on her chest, waiting for him to do whatever it is he is going to do. The way the maze is set up, those six hundred poles are set close enough together that nothing the size of a horse is going to get through. There is only one way in and one way out. "Damn interference," she thinks. "Three days, Pigeon, what are they doing to my stallion?" She goes to the *Dreamtime* pole where Pigeon is perched in her mind. "Got any Shiraz?" she thinks to ask. "It's liable to be awhile."

Now this horse is a thinker. He hits a dead end, blocked by a post. He backs up and tries another path, up jumps another post. He puts his haunches in rewind and tries to find the path that's going to take him to that manger of timothy and sweet molasses oats he sees now for the first time, this is going to be no quick lunch. It is a battle of wits between labyrinth and horse, each having their own design on the walk of life, their reputation not gauged by how well they are built, but how well they apply their mental gears.

He's there! A *gentle* reminder it's time for some oats. He lets out a soft nicker, communicating to Vi, "I have arrived." For all of that, he will receive whatever treat Vi has left him, but not much pampering. The real reward is the individual return from the trip is with a higher IQ.

One nun in her nineties is shuffling along behind a walker. Some nuns are using canes to balance their sisterly act. Just a few are in wheelchairs, but not one of them in this community is fitted with a hip replacement, and most nuns are walking on their own sturdy legs without the help of walking aids.

The gerontologists are at The Orchard of Retreat studying why the Sisters do remarkably well as they get older, having the moral support of quiet faith. These nuns are volunteering to take a battery of tests as research subjects in a unique study to determine how some women age better than others, the latter-day convent being a perfect place to study aging, because all of the nuns have had similar backgrounds. Each has spent her life eating pretty much the same healthy foods, getting similar educations, and working similar careers, shunning cigarettes, alcohol, marriage, sex, and childbirth. With these lifestyle variables canceled out, it is easier to figure out which biological factors make the difference between those who age quickly and those who don't.

While longer lives are not necessarily better lives, the study has already led to the discovery that memory loss and dementia that afflicts the nuns with Alzheimer's may be due to tiny, unnoticed strokes, suggesting that many strokes may be preventable with something as simple as taking an aspirin a day, further suggesting that Alzheimer's may very well be an unstoppable disease, not by curing it, but by preventing the strokes that do the bulk of the damage.

"She has a good complexion and a sweet expression," Sister Pino says of Julie Burnside. Sister Pino came from St. Michael's Mission near Window Rock, capital of Navajo Nation. The Mission School thrives on the Navajo Reservation thanks to the generosity of Katharine Mary Drexel, who, in 1885, was a twenty-six-year-old Philadelphia socialite. Katharine and her two sisters, Elizabeth and Louise inherited 14 million dollars from their father, banker Francis Drexel. He said his daughters would control the money even if they were to marry, but marriage and money meant little to them at the time.

One day, two priests came to see the sisters Drexel and they appointed Katharine to go downstairs to speak with them. They explained to Katharine that out West, an impoverished and mistreated Indian population suffered. Their existence was in jeopardy and they had no knowledge of Christianity.

The priests knew that schools needed to be built and missionaries needed to educate the Indian youths, but to do so would require money, and that's what led them to the

Drexel parlor. The wealthy family was known for its charity among Philadelphia's poor. Devout Catholics, the Drexel's believed their fortune had been brought to them from God to help the needy.

Katharine — the fairest of the three sisters — was expected to assume the role of a society wife, but she wanted to serve God in a different way. She and her sisters agreed to provide funds for the mission building in the West. Eventually, Katharine left her lavish life and entered a Catholic convent.

She established a new order in 1891, and professed her vows as the first nun of the Sisters of the Blessed Sacrament for Indians and Colored People, taking the name Mary Katharine. In 1896, she purchased two hundred acres the Navajos called Tsehohotso, about two miles from Window Rock.

A building was built to house three Brothers to preach the word of God, but who soon realized that the Navajos couldn't understand their language. Along with two teenage Navajo boys, they created a Navajo dictionary, and soon the Navajo got used to hearing their native words spoken by the brown-cloaked men and grew to trust them.

Katharine headed West in 1900 to oversee the building of the St. Michael Indian School and soon Sisters arrived to staff the school. She continued to establish schools for American Indians and African-Americans. She gave up her leadership and retired to a contemplative atmosphere just like the Sisters here at The Orchard of Retreat. She contracted pneumonia and died at the age of ninety-six.

Today, with the help of her carefully invested fortune, the Sisters of the Blessed Sacrament still run the St. Michael Indian School. Mass is said daily and on weekends in the parish church — which seats about a hundred and fifty, the same amount of seats in the Church of Pish. In the spring and summer, the church's front lawn is populated with flowers and vegetables and there is a fast-flowing artesian well comparable to the artesian well and jujube trees on the formerly known as Pish Convent property.

St. Michael's Indian Mission School is the oldest still-operating school on the Navajo Reservation thanks to Katharine Drexel's old-day vision and generosity.

The Orchard of Retreat — a haven for the aging nun community — now has a chance to endure that same century-old leadership, thanks to Mercedes Cade's modern-day generosity and Violet Mace-Reese's conservation vision.

Whether you call it good fortune, chance meeting, twist of fate, or the miracle work of the Divine Providence, the fork in the road goes back as far as 1879 to a historic spot in northern Arizona called Mormon Crossing. Here, you can cross Chevelon Creek, where Mormons from Brigham City graded a road and homesteaded the spot now called Mormon Crossing. Those homesteads were eventually abandoned because the creek didn't provide enough water to irrigate the crops, but today, wild mulberry, tall black walnut trees, and huge cottonwoods grow in abundance.

Mormon Crossing, St. Michael's Indian Mission School, The Pish Convent, The Orchard of Retreat; at first, they may have been historical toil for survival, random kindness, a 3,250-pipe-organ dream and meditative contemplation that all grew into great-hearted decisions that made positive differences in lives.

It's the kind of thing that inspires authors to write books.

Horses are not like other livestock. They need training to be safe to work around and they need a considerable amount of gentleness to be salable. Whoever heard of a fancy heifer having to be halter-broke? Cows are bred for their femininity and broodiness, with an emphasis on reproductive qualities. This isn't done so much in horses. Horses are athletes and buyers look for athletic mares. Even race horse buyers expect a yearling to be halter-broke.

The man introduces himself as Justin Trevor Malone. Says he is a jockey's agent. Says most fans don't even know jockeys agents exist. He tells who they are, what they do, and why. They are a jockey's publicity person, bill collector, spotter, and bookkeeper. They keep track of the horses the jockeys ride in what race, watch for odd traits in a horse's workouts spotting things sometimes the trainers don't. It gives them bargaining power when they talk to the trainers and if the jockey can show improvement, the agent can keep the jockey in work. All trainers want winners, but very few horses are instant winners. They have to go through a period of development.

It's also the agent's responsibility to keep track of what is owed to the jockey in purse and mount fees, and since most are traveling jockeys, the agent arranges hotel reservations, plane and car transportation, and meals.

Justin Trevor Malone says he is scouting a young horse for a buyer and the jockey he represents on the Ruidoso Downs circuit. They have nothing against horse racing, but Vi and Sadie think not — commercialism prevails at the racetrack. We see that compassion seldom can survive in the S and two whiskers of a dollar sign. And when you think about the force-stream hydrotherapy treatment, the sore horse — after two or three days of treatment — can get back on the track and run a good race. It's the opinion of the owner and trainer, but an interested observer has quite another opinion after seeing the Jacuzzi concept, a thirty-minute water massage with the horse's feet in a bubble bucket. This person sees that the horse is still wobbly on its legs. In this person's opinion, there is no curative value of hydrotherapy and is just masking long-term pain and lameness is predicted.

A race horse spends most of its time in a barn. This is not what Vi and Sadie wants for their foals. Justin Trevor Malone goes away, scratching his head wondering why. He offered them top dollar.

Anyway, discipline means the difference between good and poor sport. Extreme care must be given to insure the horses are not taxed beyond their endurance and all animals need to be carefully brought up to a fine fitness before any activity. After all, there would be no cutting horse activities without cows or race horses without jockeys. Without lineage, the fillies may or may not have made good race horses. Who knows what mix of stallions mounted what mix of mares in the desert? Originally descended from Spanish conquistador ponies, the wild mustangs are a rainbow of chestnuts, bays, roans, sorrels, appaloosas, quarter horses, thoroughbreds, and draft horses.

Vi gets all choked up and says, "To me, they're the greatest living horses I'm ever going to see. And I know I can't take but half the credit, half of that coil of fuse is yours, hon, but I am partly responsible for caring for something created from *Sagebrush Rebellion*."

It takes time and a whole lot of patience, and a world of try, but in the end, it's been worth the effort. And you know a feeling like this sets a woman up for a long time.

Nailheads, brass tacks, wagon-wheel chair arms, Western motifs of saddles, cactus, and Native American weavings upholstered on the bright-dyed leather sofa and chair backs take us back to the ranch furniture of the '30s, '40s, and '50s, in yellows, blues, reds, and greens. Remember this wonderful frontier furniture?

Brock & Morrow-Bate Tannery still uses the same techniques and equipment that was there when the tannery was founded in 1873. The employees still turn out just a hundred and fifty hides or "sides" as they are called each week. The perfect hides are Sadie's and Vi's. They are aniline dyed; the color completely penetrates the hide and no chemical protectants are used. Their full-grain hides are not sanded, nor do they need to be sprayed or pasted to cover up scars.

This leather they have grown is considered pristine, but then, so is the thousand-and-some acres the cows have to openly graze. Some would say you don't grow leather, but Sadie and Vi will argue that. When you plant something on your acres – or in this case, transplant it – and tend to it in hopes of harvesting it one day, you are *growing* it. Sadie and Vi planted these cows not from seeds, but from four-legged bovine dreams with perfect hides to make quality ranch furniture. What they have here is a leather ranch, not a cattle ranch. The main purpose is growing leather, but first, the cows go to the slaughter house to harvest the meat that Sadie and Vi donate to the women's shelter. The exact size and shape of the finished leather is dictated by the size and shape of the cow hide that the tannery receives from the meat packing company. There is no waste in this outfit.

Not a day passes without Sadie and Vi watching over their cows and outfit. And they watch it from under their night's blankets. In the morning, they come back in a different form. They survey the ranch, checking out the whereabouts of their cows and they keep an eye on the grasses they planted making sure they don't overgraze.

This leather ranch is a place where Western heritage is kept alive. Sadie and Vi keep diaries of the modern-day frontier woman and pen manuscripts on every aspect of the

Western life. The manuscript is getting thick. There will be many leather-covered volumes that tell about life in the saddle, the land, the wildlife, and the weather. They can fill one manuscript just telling about their windmill. When one or the other of them straps on their holster and grease gun, you very well better believe that twice a week when they climb the twenty-foot tower, fighting off wasps and getting splinters, they are also lubricating cowgirl sexuality, ever-going, everlasting, and guaranteed not to wreck in any storm that does not destroy buildings. This says something in the vernacular about the comparison of a sturdy windmill to that of a woman's secure sexuality: in that the winds of change are ever-growing and pioneered by the strong ones — those women who went before us. Does it make you wonder when it's going to blow through your town? Vi hears it. She looks up at the weather vanes; this time hearing the other *vain* – it can't be — Andy Sue!

This fucking rock of a woman is obsessed with gallantry!

"A ranch! It might as well be Australia, Violet!" Andy Sue says, climbing off her Harley.

"It is Australia, Andy Sue — *Dreamtime*," Vi says. "Come inside."

"Here — I brought your favorite shade of lipstick," Andy Sue says. Andy Sue gave one of Vi's political contacts a free year's membership at the club to pull some strings with the Department of Motor Vehicles to find Vi's whereabouts. It's the same way Vi found Sadie — through a contact that had pull with the DMV. So when Andy Sue said before Vi could ask, "I found you through the DMV," Vi couldn't very well say it wasn't a good idea.

The words came from under the seat of the deacon's bench. "Andy Sue — this is Sadie Cade, my cowgirl," Vi introduces the two of them. And she says it so damn proud.

"Nice to meet you, Andy Sue," Sadie greets, handing Andy Sue a bottle of beer. "Looks like you could use this."

"Thanks," Andy Sue says, looking at her watch. "I'm on Montana time — happy hour." Andy Sue isn't herself. She looks weathered, Vi thinks. And there seems to be no artificialities or buffed attitude, or even that she is here in a vainglory attempt to rescue her obsession. She isn't here for arm candy.

"What brings you out of your element, Andy Sue?" Vi asks. "You're a long way from home." Something is really bothering Andy Sue. She isn't living in present-moment vainglory or in the oxygen-enriched pay-off of a workout.

"I'm bored, Violet — tired of living with the sweat," Andy Sue cries. Vi hasn't seen a rock cry since Blue Buffalo. She breaks down in Vi's arms, with Sadie looking at it. It is sad. This is no time for jealousy. It is most obvious that Andy Sue needs Violet. She is under some kind of psychological collapse. Giving an ear to others is indicative of how much love you have for yourself.

Vi shows Andy Sue to the bathroom to freshen up. She brushes out Andy Sue's tangled hair, then leaves her a basin of warm water and squeezes a lemon on a fresh washcloth.

"She's beautiful, just like you said, but I wasn't expecting crumbling limestone — something more like granite," Sadie whispers.

"I don't know what's knocked her off her rock, hon. Thanks for being nice. She seems so lost, and she's so far away from home. I'm surprised she made it this far on her bike. She's not balanced enough to even be riding it," Vi says. "Do you have any suggestions as to how I can comfort her and find out what's caused her breakdown?"

"Yes, I think you should take her to the paint mine, spend the night," Sadie answers. "Saddle up Painted Maiden for her to ride. My pony's good on her feet in times of ceremony.

Remember where we found her, with the Indians, so you take Andy Sue to our Indian paint mine."

"You know Andy Sue and I were in a relationship, cowgirl. I'm not sure it's wise to be alone with her," Vi says with concern. "I'm not chiseled out of stone — I'm soft when it comes to a woman in need."

"Do what you have to with her. It's a natural way of living," Sadie says. "I know what kind of atmosphere you'll be in — been there with you in the passionate shadows of a bush telly at *Dreamtime*. Make her see new light with what has become stale for her. I know who my cowgirl is. I'll be here when you get back. The oil lamp will be filled and the wick trimmed. I like myself too much to apologize for sending you off with her."

Vi takes Andy Sue out to the barn and saddles up Mavericka Bonanza and Painted Maiden. Andy Sue climbs atop Painted Maiden and Vi adjusts the stirrups to fit Andy Sue, then ties on the bedrolls with strips of rawhide lacing. They do the whole thing up the way Sadie suggested, except for one thing. Now there are times in a woman's life where she has no need to have things fit into others' perceptions of how it ought to be. If it doesn't work or accomplish any good, she simply says, "It's alright, we tried something different." It is simply abandoned and not regretted, so with this in mind, Andy Sue — with a leg fit comfortably on each side of Painted Maiden and Sadie astride Vi's palomino, Mavericka Bonanza, both ponies outfitted with martingales, and olives in their saddlebags — set out for the paint mine. Things at this point have drastically changed. Vi stayed. It will be her filling the oil lamp and trimming the wick. Questionable? Does there have to be an explanation? Perhaps some will need to find an answer. Those will be the insecure ones who are probably searching for certainty and have a fear of the unknown. Those will be the ones who need to go in search of a restored windmill.

The paint mine is a few miles out on their thousandth acre. The colored clays were once mined by the prehistoric Indians for use as ceremonial body paint. The colors are caused by various iron oxides, yellow limonite, and red hematite mixed with sediment. Erosion exposes layers stained by bands of bright yellow, ocher, brick red, shades of pink and mauve, and pure white.

Several spearheads have been found here and after close inspection, it isn't hard to dream of Indians separating and milling the tinted clays into paints to appease their gods.

Upon her first thought — when Sadie readily gave her permission to Vi to bring Andy Sue to the paint mine — she pointed out to Vi that her decision was based on the fact the clay had not been taken from the paint mine in nearly a century. Given the natural processes of erosion and time to remove old scars, saying perhaps Andy Sue needs to experience this same natural way of softening without damaging her chiseled beauty. So Sadie is going to show Andy Sue all about the soft clay that lies beneath a hard layer of white, cross-bedded sandstone, which makes for a balanced rock. The paint mine is a strata of metaphor embedded with crystals of gypsum.

"What is this place?" Andy Sue asks, looking up at the capstones, pedestals, and arches.

"An old Indian paint mine. Here, the Indians mined the rocks for the colors to make their body paint."

Andy Sue acts like she might be capable of appreciating the scenic quality and beauty of the multi-hued walls. "Is there a treasure at the end of the rainbow?" she asks.

"That treasure can be the imagined spirits and totems of a vanished culture or the treasure can be the pastels of solitude," Sadie answers. They are here just before the sun is going down. "I'm going to tell you something, Andy Sue. Only three other people know. That would be Vi, my mother, and my attorney, and I'd like to keep it that way. I'm a wealthy woman, won fifteen million in the lottery. That is no treasure compared to this. Just wait until you see it when the moon comes up. The canyon walls twinkle with a sparkling, silver glitter on a clear night. And when you see it tonight, Andy Sue — that's when the magic begins."

"I need some magic. I sold my gym. Did Violet tell you I owned a gym?" Andy Sue asks. It chokes her up.

"Yes, she mentioned it. Did you tell Vi you sold the gym?"

"No, she saddled up the horses and I assumed it was her that was taking me for a ride. I was going to tell her on the trail."

"Tell me, Andy Sue. Tell me things *I* need to know. I'm going to light up a bush telly to soften things up," Sadie says.

"What's a bush telly?" Andy Sue asks.

"Australia's campfire."

"Violet said something about this being Australia. What's that about, cowgirl?"

"Vi and I are converts from the Mormon faith to Australia's *Dreamtime*. Places where we go — stories from the Sky Heroes, the supernatural Aboriginal ancestors," Sadie explains. "You can build a whole religion around it. Everyone you meet in a *Dreamtime* story will know one another. They're having a bit of drama. *Dreamtime* converts pursue life as they see it. Andy Sue, do you want to go *Dreamtime*?"

"Convert?" Andy Sue asks. "Well, I'm having a bit of drama. I came to apologize to Violet. You know she was my wife, cowgirl? I lost her because I was living in vain, pumping iron and worshipping a baptismal font of mineral oil — shallow religion, isn't it, cowgirl?"

"Buffed, pretty warrioress, self-chiseled rock of a woman, I'd say that's a damn strong religion, took a lot of self-discipline to create that goddess, Andy Sue, but there's a different way to look at it out here in the New Mexico outback. You can find your soul and soften your edges without crumbling your chiseled beauty the gym created, converting to the softer rock broken down into colorful sands and clays. The red ocher would be the one you're looking for — it's one of the weathered compounds of iron, the same stuff you're made of. Look at it, it's all here: the things that matter the most, friendship, healing, softening, beauty, courtship, *love*." Sadie reaches for Andy Sue's hand, soft as a rabbit's paw. "You've got soft palms for such a hard outline."

"From the powder to grip the barbells," Andy Sue whispers.

"Why are you whispering?" Sadie asks.

"You've softened me some." Andy Sue knows this isn't about setting out on a sidewalk in a plastic armchair attracting looks. Such adventures appease only the vain, fishing for compliments to reel in their ego. She hasn't figured out what kind of bait cowgirl is using, but she is beginning to feel the lure. "My dream used to be to get ahead of the local competition."

"What's your dream now, Andy Sue?" Sadie asks. "Tell me."

"Give me one."

"Nervous or aroused?" Sadie smiles, seeing the woman before her fidget.

"Both," Andy Sue answers, stumped that she is managing to pull herself together.

"You're feeling the convert. It works a strange magic on some women in their forties. They buy mini skirts, change jobs, wear gold, and disappear with exotic female dancers, some even carry it on well into their fifties, but beneath the surface, all is not well," Sadie says. "Something happens — it happened to you."

"That hits home — wherever *that* is," Andy Sue wonders.

"Maybe *here*, Andy Sue," Sadie says. "You're one of the smart ones — you bought *Dreamtime*." Sadie takes Andy Sue to *Dreamtime* just over the Tropic of Capricorn. She chooses to tell Andy Sue just the right story, the story of S'ledge and the Emu Bush.

"The woman we are going to visit is S'ledge. She moved new to the outback. Camels hauled her house in pieces.

"She set the house over an emu bush, cut a hole in the floorboards so it could live inside. S'ledge catered to the emu bush for all the good it was going to do her. She became so entangled up in the emu bush she could see nothing else, not the soft, clean sand of Yagga Yagga, not the deep sandstone gorges of Pilbara, not the botanical walkabout.

"Growing, growing, and growing more, the emu bush covered her windows (don't you hate that?) forcing S'ledge to choose between the emu bush or her good friend, the spirited one who wrote S'ledge heartfelt letters of poetry and wisdom. She chose to lock her friend out, instead living lonely and cold, hiding her life behind the emu bush, like it was controlling her, poisoning her, making her choose (her or me).

"S'ledge's story illustrates the letdowns and heartbreaks life can inflict," Sadie said. "So this is what happened."

"I'm listening," Andy Sue whispers. She is picking up on it — where *everyone you meet in a Dreamtime story will know one another*.

"One hot day, the beekeeper was hauling his hives by truck to pollinate sunflowers. Tire blew out from the heat, the truck rolled over spilling the hives, bees headed straight to S'ledge's house. They moved inside getting in through the mean cracks caused by the gloating emu bush pushing out everything that lived large and happy.

"Stung her bloody, made her curse, but what was worse, she walked across the road to the house of the one who used to be her friend to get a compassionate poultice for the welts, never minding how she had pushed her away, but her friend didn't answer the door. Perhaps she was out on a *National Geographic* botanical walkabout looking at dried billybuttons in the talcum-fine sand the color of paprika, fields of lilac *pussy*tails, gathering bush bananas and wild onions, stopping off at age-old rock carvings of circles and tracks near a waterhole where the kangaroos, emus, and wild turkeys watered. Entangled with an emu bush once herself, the friend knew very well the manipulating ways of the emu bush. It killed cows on the spot if they ate it; it killed off a woman's spirit too.

"One day, at the end of the dry season just before the wet ..."

"What's the ending, cowgirl?" Andy Sue asks. On rare occasions, Sadie doesn't recite *Dreamtime* endings. She just leaves it dangling like a crumbling rock about to plunge its way off the cliff into soft sand.

"Oh, there is no real ending, it's all chiseled in the mind, not in the books," Sadie says. She wants Andy Sue to really think about this one.

"No ending!"

"Some say S'ledge never did get herself free of the emu bush and it smothered her. Some say lightning ignited a bush fire and it spread to S'ledge's house. She couldn't get out because the emu bush had her trapped and there was no way out for her. They say her family took her ashes to Barossa Valley in South Australia and spread them over the Shiraz vines heavy with grapes, by stout Lutheran churches built by German settlers many vintages ago. See that soft powder by your feet, Andy Sue? It's red ocher that's crumbled into sand from a *Dreamtime* cliffhanger. Ocher and ochre: two spellings. What do *you* think happened to S'ledge?"

Andy Sue picked up a pinch of the red ocher and rubbed it between her fingertips. "It's soft," she says, "and home," thinking for a minute. "I think S'ledge apologized to her friend and got rid of the emu bush."

"You would know that best," Sadie said, and then they took a soft dirt nap into the night, that is all.

Last night, Sadie showed Andy Sue the magic of the paint mine. The sky is deeper and the moon and stars brighter than anyplace you can imagine. Sadie raved about the tranquility. Andy Sue learned where *Dreamtime* converts store their metaphors when they're not using them. You want magic? The New Mexico outback is thick with it. These are real women living their daily lives. They are religiously and culturally private and they open their land only to a chosen few who are in need. Those would be the converts.

"Everybody's working on something, Andy Sue — hides, ranch furniture, spearheads, mustangs — what are you working on, huh?" Vi asks.

"The convert and the cowgirl," Andy Sue says so damn proud. "I'm sorry for pushing you out of my life, Violet. I should have held on to you. It only comes around once in a lifetime, if you're lucky. You don't know what you've lost until it's not there anymore."

"You want to buy this little filly, Andy Sue?" Vi asks.

"And do what with her?"

"Tame her and find her gentle spirit. Put some of that softened muscle to work here at the ranch. Try it for a while, and if you don't find your Marlboro spirit, then you can move on, but at least see what it is we do here," Vi offers with sincerity. She's never really got over Andy Sue — she just moved on. Never caught up in the politics of Andy Sue, all the legislation in the world cannot abolish kissing her, so she throws her coil of fuse and caution to the wind and kisses Andy Sue. "Now you owe Sadie one," Vi says, mounting Mavericka Bonanza, riding off letting the wind comb her hair, "and tell her I said so!"

"Where'd you go after you left the gym?" Andy Sue hollers.

"To paint a duck!"

Andy Sue picks up a pitchfork and pitches a few forks of timothy, trading a baptismal font of mineral oil for a hay manger.

Time slips away.

Andy Sue is seeking inspiration, letting her eyes drift over the "Christmas scenes displayed on the cards." How ironic that Christmas cards are sent by 99 percent of people who live in non-agricultural areas, but their cards depict pictures of animals and fields and clean skies. These cowgirls live Christmas everyday — modern-day feminist shepherds tending to their flock. It is the cowgirl who looks over the barn and maintains the mangers. Andy Sue takes it all in — the baby calf and the Border collie and those cool folk art weather vanes, and the horse-drawn team pulling a coach. The other two mustang fillies went to a gentle young man with proud blue eyes and talented hands — Jediah, Son of Moses and Zea, but you knew that, right? Their identical J-monogrammed foreheads chose their destiny from the minute they got their wobbly-leg start, that being pulling the Lord's wheel.

For the better part of the year, Jediah has immersed himself in wagon building and restoration. He has completed his home school studies and received his diploma.

He makes wagons, making sure the wheels turn, the hand brakes can be set and released, tool boxes can be opened and closed, carriage lanterns flash on and off, and he makes sure the burlap bean sacks are filled to the double-stitched seam and sewn shut as standard equipment and not an option.

Jediah's carriage factory showroom has a line of horse-drawn vehicles made up and waiting to be customized with the buyer's choice of color, upholstery, top, and other options. The trusting buyer — before putting down any deposit money and relying on the carriage maker's reputation, hoping the carriage maker lived up to it, here — can stop off in the showroom and inspect the iron-rimmed wheels, sit on the driver's seat, squint at the undercarriage, and look at the overall lines assuring it will last beyond the first parade and hold up on the trail. And, if the buyer has brought along the horses and harness that is going to pull it, and is willing to wait until a shaft is attached, they're welcome to test drive it to see how solid Jediah's reputation is. He throws the sermon in for free.

Only when he's talking about the Lord's quality in his construction, Jediah shows his enthusiasm. He squats down and caresses the underbelly, saying proudly, "They're made from an old, laborious method," and then he goes on to the sermon that is not weak or plywood preachy. "I've seen folks break right in two, from things that weaken their carriage. You see this surrey here? It's here because it's weak, that's why the owner brought it in to be strengthened. That owner is standing right over there," he points to one of his converts.

"Amen, Brother, I'm here at the Lord's wheel because I am weak, too," he says, giving his testimonial. "This young man says you learn by doing. He tells me I need to get a vocation. He says you end up with a better vehicle in this House of the Lord's wheel, so I'm listening to what he has to offer. So far, Brother Jediah has shown me three models, all of which hold up after adaptations and improvements. I'm satisfied with his knowledge."

"This surrey is cut down to allow easy access to the seats. There's no sit-down money here for any able-bodied adult — I'm talking about welfare. Now the Lord wants us to have an easy life, but, in this case, to those who give in, it weakens the carriage because the sideboard should be bolted to the sill to form a truss. This is where it will break in two. We employ a sturdy metal brace and tie it into the seat, *no plywood*," Jediah says, "there's not a scrap of plywood in any of my carriages — they're not going to give in, they're sturdy. They need to be — your grandkids will be driving it one day with the Lord at the reins."

Jediah is not only popular with the older crowd, but he has a following with the skateboarders. They ride on his every word. He gets intense with the teenagers not much younger than him, using carriage speak regarding their actions and behavior. "I don't use roller bearings in wheel hubs. I use the old boxing and spindle. If a carriage rolls too easy, it tends to overrun the team and they're always fighting. That's what you are — a team, right? Wears the team out and the driver, too. If a hub is well greased, there's very little friction and wear." He reminds them that the carriages have always been the only method of transportation of the Amish, so they have to build them right. This causes all the skateboarders to flip their skateboards over and inspect their models, comparing manufacturers. It teaches them about quality control and that usually takes teamwork.

Jediah can find a sermon in almost anything. He's about turning wheels, not pages. To him, the wagons represent a link to the time when ranching and farming was a way of life where transportation was equine and wagons were the only way to move supplies. They're a part of important history. When the time comes, he'll make a convert out of you.

Sadie Cade's first attempt to meet her Marlboro spirit, before Violet Mace-Reese came to join her, came through braiding horsehair, one of the oldest arts of civilization.

That's what the "coil of feminist fuse" is made from. Can you believe that? Each time Sadie and Vi throw the coil of feminist fuse, they are throwing a swatch of braided horsehair to the wind. Sadie buys it by the pound in black, white, and brown, and she braids it. To throw a coil of feminist fuse is

From The Convent To The Rawhide

to bring land and woman together. Their love for the coil of feminist fuse runs as deep as the windmill sucker rod.

Same goes for *Dominga Rio of Cuero* — who is braiding the Judas's mane — and the Polish woman at the Christmas tree plantation — who climbs a peeled spruce-log ladder and sits in a ten-foot-high rocking chair braiding horsehair as she watches over the growth — and the Sherpa woman — who climbs Mt. Everest — and *The Buckskin Skirt Oar Traveler* and *Winonah: First-born Daughter*. Their love for braided horsehair, the coil of feminist fuse speaks volumes.

When you've spent too much time being impatient and too much time being rushed or pushed by interferences that have nothing to do with real living, do what these women do — braid some horsehair and throw it to the wind. You can even light it with a match — but if you do, nothing will ever be the same. This isn't a warning — it's a suggestion: take off and see what else you can find.

Make yourself comfortable. Get some spicy beef jerky, tie on a pink bandanna if you like (it's optional), but you damn well better get a squaw-hold on the reins, you've graduated to braided rawhide if you've come this far.

There's no turning back.

The Judas is outrunning a wildfire in Colorado. Bobcat Gulch has exploded into flames. Some say they spotted him on Storm Mountain. The handler turned him out of the stock trailer a couple of days ago for a mustang roundup and that's the last the outfit has seen of him. The runners abandoned the roundup after seeing the fire heading straight to the funnel.

He isn't working the funnel this time. It's a death trap. He is working a narrow, rocky ravine known as Bobcat Gulch, turning the wilds back away from the burlap where the fire has spread to.

The smoke is thick, rolling low. Mustangs like any other animal are instinctual. The Judas lets out a series of whinnies, the *Judas Code*. ._.._ (Hoof it) _ _. . . . _ _ (Fire!) ____ . . . ___ _ (Outlaw Red). The wilds follow the Code that will probably save their lives. The Judas can smell burning horsehair, but he doesn't panic.

The roan mare that has become an inspiration for the herd has fallen trying to swish out fire on her tail she picked up from a burning bush. She just lays there on the ground knowing she doesn't have long. She lost the fire when she hit the dirt, but the smoke is filling her lungs. She isn't in any pain. Her legs are fine, not broken, but she is stressed and exhausted and doesn't have the strength to get up.

Now the Judas knows he can't turn back for the roan, but he gets ideas, this is no time for horsing around. He doesn't know the layout of the land, he's been brought to Colorado near Estes Park where he is needed, but he's seen this same rocky terrain before, in New Mexico, in Arizona, and in Utah. The wilds favor the same habitat in these states, some terrain flatter than others, but the land almost always has some rough, rocky terrain. It's why the wilds pick it, they know they won't be bothered by human interlopers.

He can hear the ancient conifer trees popping and cracking, fueled by forty-mile-per hour winds and when he sees the eighty-foot fire-breathing dragon, he knows he doesn't have much time to slay the dragon, be a hero. He's not been in a worse situation than this and he thinks to himself, "What are we, Judas, but withers, loins, shoulders, crests, polls, forelocks, hocks, hindquarters, flanks, bellies, stifles, fetlocks, and hooves — framework across the West for the equine convert?"

From The Convent To The Rawhide

He takes off like some wild ass and independent politician, letting the wind comb his mane, his heartbeat goes from twenty-five beats per minute to a hundred beats per minute at full gallop through the smoke which has now turned from black to gray-green, never minding the firebrands, pieces of burning wood being lobbed by the wind. He prays his hind cannons, midway up from his tired hooves have some climb left in them — he's got to make it up to the highest rock outcropping where he can see blue sky. *Climb, climb, climb*, pick it up boy, *up, up, up*, get a foothold. The Judas rears up on his hind legs, then stamps out the *Judas Code.* _ . . _ . . _ . . _ _ _ _ _ _ _ _ _ S.O.S! . . . (Save our spirit). _ . . _ . . _ _ _ _ _ _ _ S.O.S!

To those not familiar with the extreme intelligence of the mustang and its spirit of adventure, it is because of its wild heritage and the danger of losing the bloodline that self-spurs the Judas to risk his own life, ascending to the top of the perilous rock outcropping to round up an S.O.S. signal to the one in the big sky — the slurry pilot.

The four-engine aircraft flies over and sees the Judas rear up like a scene in a Western movie. "What the hell!" the pilot wonders. "You're one bold Windy Cochise. Is this what you want, Cochise?" The pilot makes a left bank and lets it loose, the slurry of fire-suppression chemical. He radios to the other slurry pilot. "Timber Wolf, Timber Wolf, copy? This is the Raven."

"Copy, Raven, go ahead."

"If I didn't know better, I just saw a mustang on top of something you wouldn't believe. This Windy Cochise looked like a bronze sculpture, but he wasn't glued down. He had less room on that crag to stand on than the base of a sculpture, and he was sturdy on his feet! Drop your load in Bobcat Gulch, just in case he was asking. I'd swear to it, Timber Wolf, Out."

"Copy, Raven, Out."

Now the Judas's powers have limits. He knows not to tax himself beyond his potential. He feels good about things, he's going back for the roan mare, wake her up from her dirt nap before night falls when there is a danger of falling snags and night winds that wake smoldering fires. The roan feels his sweaty muzzle caress her muzzle and she opens her eyes, glazed over with fire ash, thinking she surely must have died and went through the burlap gates with bronze sculptures of the Judas glued down on the gateposts, Hero of the Wilds.

Every year, entrants in the annual Federal Duck Stamp Competition compete for the right to have their waterfowl art on a stamp. The Duck Stamp is required by all waterfowl hunters. All duck hunters know about the Duck Stamps — you buy one with your hunting license.

The signed Duck Stamp is an interesting hunting souvenir, but the same *unsigned* stamp is a valuable collectible that rises in value hundreds of times over. What makes these unsigned stamps so valuable is that very few are printed, and many states destroy any unsold stamps at the end of the hunting season. Funds collected from the sale of the stamp supports waterfowl conservation, in some states, the funds are used for acquisition of waterfowl habitat which includes the habitat of the cinnamon teal.

Congratulations to Vi Montana, this year's recipient of the Federal Duck Stamp Competition. She was doing a lot more in that cozy Montana loft than painting a teal. She was reconnecting with conservation through "canvas politics."

America is still influenced by Western frontier experiences and birds and animals are tied to the human experience. Vi

From The Convent To The Rawhide

doesn't have to count every feather to be a successful, accepted artist. You can see the motion in the puddle and feel the breeze swaying the swamp grass.

Wildlife artists have benefited for many years from the growth of the conservation movement. In 1934, the U.S. Government began a wetlands program. The idea was to require hunters of migratory birds to buy a federal stamp. The money was to be used to purchase and maintain habitat for the birds. These stamps have had a lasting impact on wildlife art, providing a showcase for many artists who are among the most successful wildlife painters.

This is the day when the sticks come down. The mustangs have conquered the labyrinth and each one of them has found their tame gray shape, each one at their own pace. The poles of the labyrinth will stay, always, as a spiritual contribution.

Vi is emotional. A lot of spiritual things went on in this circle — things she will never forget. The sticks have in the same way found their tame gray shapes — you know how wood bleaches to gray when it is exposed to the sun and how moisture shapes its personality from cracks and weathered slivers?

"What motivated her?" Andy Sue asks Sadie. They are watching from a distance to give Vi time to reflect.

"*Sagebrush Rebellion*," Sadie answers, and she says it so damn proud. "Nothing's been the same since we lit the fuse."

"Carnival's left town, cowgirls. I'm inviting you to a bonfire tonight for a celebration — will you join me?" Vi asks.

"What can I bring?" Andy Sue asks.

"Sadie," Vi winks.

"What can I bring, cowgirl?" Sadie asks.

"Your mattress tags — we'll burn them with the sticks," Vi says, even more of a social rebel these days, a shrugger, resisting enculturation and meaningless policies.

There are different types of knowledge — that of books, that of art, and that of wizened women. When an educated woman turns forty, she gains five years of knowledge overnight. It can be better explained like this.

"How smart are you, cowgirl?" Sadie asks Vi at the bonfire.

"I reckon I be 'bout as smart as yellow dots on gray skin," Vi replies, then takes off her gray midriff with yellow snap buttons and throws it on top of the burning sticks that have served their purpose. "Tribal matchsticks in a bonfire always warm the spirit. The flames of many tribes burn bright tonight. So glad the tribes shared their sticks, guiding the mustangs to their gentle spirit," Vi says. She gets all choked up watching the sticks burn to embers. "It's time for a new dream."

"Make no little plans, they have no magic to stir a cowgirl's blood," Sadie says. She says it often.

Andy Sue has a lot of catching up to do — Pigeon's War, Ten Thousand Village, Spanish moss at Muleshoe, cornfield maze, quarry, auction bidding card, greasing the windmill, braiding horsehair, mustang roundup, filling the oil lamp, trimming the wick! Turning forty! The list goes on and on, a cowgirl's work is never done.

"Let's call it a night, girls," Sadie says, hosing down the embers. "We've got some old boards to salvage in the morning."

Round nails didn't come into use until about 1890. They are salvaging an old spirits cellar that had the hand-forged square nails, salvaging those precious nails as well. What wonderful old-day rusty spikes to hold together modern-day ranch furniture to lasso in the look with a natural Western element that accentuates the trail mix of ranch furniture — leather, rope, wood, and iron.

It takes a trained eye to locate these old sites and then the owner's permission. Most of the time, the landowner will say yes, but they almost always want out of the deal a piece of rustic ranch furniture built, because it's such a unique craft.

Nature is hard on these sights, but in the application of their furniture-making, the more rustic, the better, the teeth of nature, small bites and large bites of animals chewing on the remains is no bad thing, but dry rot is, where the boards are devoid of their natural oils. These particular boards are well over a hundred years old, so you can say Sadie and Vi are making new antiques. As crazy as it sounds, these boards are well preserved. It all has to do with the elements — climate, animals, rodents, insects, and vandals.

Sadie and Vi search for long-dead rebel personalities. They're just about everywhere — you just have to change your perspective to see them. This particular whiskey cellar was a meeting place for old-day quarry workers, bachelor miners, and a lair for lusty ladies.

"Jediah would have something to say about this," Vi says. The rake is now making these salvage trips with them. Black widows are something better dealt with at a rake's length. Speaking of Jediah, there are some old, rusty wagon-bed springs at the site. The owner asked if they would mind hauling them off. Jediah will be grateful to have them.

Carefully pulling out the square heads with the nail claw and putting them in a nail keg, they speak of boom times and slack to those hell raisers happy to come here. This whiskey cellar was a place to escape the hornet's nest of public opinion the rowdy bunch had aroused in town, merrymaking well into the wee hours. The furniture that Sadie and Vi make is also story furniture. Each piece comes with a removable furniture tag that tells where the wood and other materials are salvaged from. Furniture is history and history is furniture.

This is the day when the mustangs are turned loose. Vi has conquered her spiritual IQ. She never had any intention of keeping the mustangs. They belong free, with the wind combing their manes. She hopes, though, they will stick around on their thousand-and-some acres.

The makers of movies say this is a key feminist scene of maverick independence: six stirrups filled by pretty big hand-stitched boots of three intense, free-reigning women bouncing in the saddle — each of them with a squaw-hold on the rawhide reins and a swatch of braided horsehair, staged and gripped between their lower and upper teeth, pink bandannas tied around their pretty necks and top hats cinched down — running at full throttle across the land with seven mustangs feeling their wild oats, running along beside at the maverick speed of lightning over the restored grass. Gee, the mixed grass they planted has grown up so pretty and tall, up to the horses hocks, great movie vegetation lashing in the breeze, the windmill in the foreground, the paint mine in the background, coloring the Southwest horizon in bold colors, the palette of ceremony.

Andy Sue manages to stay aboard the filly, somehow. Both of them are still green, only having walked the labyrinth a couple of times. When Andy Sue threw a saddle on her, she stood back and watched the spirited filly buck herself dizzy. She is just learning how to take the bit, a little feisty, running with the enthusiasm of a horse who knows she is enrolled in *Sagebrush Rebellion*.

From The Convent To The Rawhide

"Time to toss your coil of fuse, cowgirl — let's pick it up!" Vi hollers back to Andy Sue. They're deep into the sagebrush, waking the pheasants from their dirt nap.

"Take your lunch in the saddle, cowgirl!" Sadie hollers when one of the pheasants knocks itself out on Andy Sue's saddle horn. It is about the size of a dinner plate.

"HOLY CHRIST!" Andy Sue hollers after she tosses her coil of fuse. The filly stops short, damn near throwing her and she's thinking about this Marlboro spirit thing, thinking she's just found it. "Rawhide!" She chokes up on the reins and swishes the slack back and forth, left and right on the filly's neck. The rawhide's in her blood (that was quick) and she's just about as aroused as she can ever remember, the excitement of *Sagebrush Rebellion* has her nipples pounding under her poncho, and the girls know *good* and *well* what is happening when Andy Sue spurs her pony and fucks her cunt against the saddle horn connecting with her G-spot (yes, it *really* is there!) "I FOUND IT!" Andy Sue hollers. 'I FOUND IT! OH, UH, UH, I GOT IT, YES! YES! DANCER, PRANCER, DASHER, DONNER, VIXEN, COMET, CUPID, BLITZEN, RUDOLPH, ORGASM!"

"Go, girl!" Vi hollers. Andy Sue named every damn reindeer, and added one that was *coming,* rang her bells, the ones Vi gave her.

"Bring it home!" Sadie hollers.

If a woman wants to find her G-spot and the supposed difference between *clitoral* and *vaginal* orgasms, well then — like a modern-day Dale Evans — she will mount a horse as celebrated as Buttermilk or Painted Maiden or Maverick Bonanza or Blaze, with a well-fit saddle and ride until her vertical smile dries up and meets with the dusty sunset.

Horses have different face markings. Here's how they are named; Star, Stripe, Blaze, Bald Face, Snip, and Walleye. This is how Andy Sue came to the filly's name. She has a white blaze that runs from her nostrils to her forelock.

Andy Sue hates to admit it, but she is kind of proud of herself. She is above that *ego* stuff; she has stepped out of the vainglory gym shoes and into the cowgirl boots. Today, she has learned a little about neck reining and a whole lot about independence — and range orgasm. She learned how to control the point of orgasm, how to stop and go on and back up, and *come* independently on *her* command, and she enjoyed it, and today, she found her Marlboro spirit, in the saddle. Only a woman who has tried this can know how to ride with her sexuality; with maverick independence and the need to work herself in wide-open spaces without material things, which generally makes a woman weak and dependent. There are better things to want than money and power. Freedom is better than security. Security cripples, leads to lameness. The coil of feminist fuse gives us freedom; gives us the opportunity to ride without men to lead the way. It gives us the chance to make women friends all on our own. Sadie Cade and Vi Montana know this well — they've been from the convent to the rawhide.

On a scale of blue-ribbon, just like Vi sees mustangs superior to humans, she also sees independence superior to dependence in all relationships: with either animals and women. The disguise of dependence in some women is so convincing, a facade. The horses they used to ride. You can tell it in the width of their smile.

There is a new bonanza of psychology, to those women who want to get back in the saddle, those women who feel like they're getting their life together after wasting years pursuing things that never came to fruition, a feminist pronouncement that says a woman needs to reach a healthy level of self-esteem before putting on a cowgirl hat. One thing more: Courage, strength, stamina, and spirit weaves a common twine in the lives of modern-day cowgirls who exemplify the spirit of the Old West.

From The Convent To The Rawhide

In each of us, there is a dreamer, and a rebel, where sex and religion ride together.

THE END

CPSIA information can be obtained at www.ICGtesting.com
Printed in the USA
LVOW130240080713

341791LV00001B/18/A